THERE IS A WAY TO LIVE FOREVER

THERE IS A WAY TO LIVE FOREVER

and Other Stories

Terry Grimwood

Black Shuck Books
www.blackshuckbooks.co.uk

First published in Great Britain in 2017 by

Black Shuck Books
Kent, UK

Versions of the following stories have previously appeared in print:
Demons and Demons (Peeping Tom Magazine, 2008, subsequently in a Wicked Whispers chapbook of the same name.)
Fracture (*BFS New Horizons #5*, 2012)
There is a Way to Live Forever (*BFS New Horizons #3*, 2011)
Think Belsen (*Sein und Werden: Clandestine Encounters*, 2008, subsequently in *The Monster Book for Girls* (TheEXAGGERATEDpress).)
A Child is a Woman's (All Hallows #43, 2007)
The Higgins Technique (*Blind Swimmer*, Eibonvale Press, 2010)
Romance in D Flat (*BFS Journal Autumn 2012*)
Long Train Runnin' (*Hellfire Crossroads 5*, Midnight Street, 2015)
Jar of Flies (Disturbed Magazine, 2014)
The Devil's Eggs (*Murky Depths #12*, 2010)
Journey to the Engine of the Earth (*Where Are We Going?*, Eibonvale Press, 2012)
NM (*Bare Bones #9*, 2009)

978-1-913038-20-5

Dedicated to David Rix
Artist, writer and friend

Contents

DEMONS AND DEMONS

"I'm running away," she said, which didn't surprise me. The short black evening dress and expensive looking coat she wore were strange clothes for a hitchhiker. Her dishevelled blonde hair, smudged make-up, laddered stockings and scuffed high-heels were further giveaways.

Then she added, "From a demon," and I found myself trying to decide whether to help her or dump her then and there on the side of the A12.

I drove on. To our left, the concrete and glass city I knew to be BT's Suffolk-based main research labs, to our right, the bland Legoland of Martlesham Heath village.

"His name is Ash," my passenger offered – which didn't help.

I'd only picked her up as an experiment, to see if I could bear driving with a passenger again. Up until then, the experiment seemed to have been working.

"Where to?" I had asked. My voice sounded strange to me, hoarse, unused.

"Where are you going?"

"Hemel Hempstead, you know, near Watford."

"That'll do."

Silence for the next ten miles or so. She seemed restless, either staring straight ahead or glancing over her shoulder. Her nervousness was infectious.

"Why is this demon chasing you?" Stupid question, but I had to say something.

"He loves me." She sounded irritated, as if the answer should be obvious. Her accent was clipped, edged with ruling class superiority.

"Can he follow us? Has he got a car?" What sort did I have in mind? A red Plymouth like in the Stephen King novel?

"No...Yes." She sighed, irritated. "He hasn't got a car, but he *can* follow us."

"Can he fly?" Weak attempt at humour, though not met with the contempt it deserved.

"Yes he can."

Dump her, my head yelled. *Now.*

"Tell me about it." So much for common sense.

"You don't want to know."

"I do. Really." Unusually forthright of me. None of that enervating reticence with women I had managed to develop since my own little car journey to Hell two years ago.

Dear God, two years already...

She stared at me for a moment, as if appraising my suitability to receive whatever tale she had to tell. Then she sighed, leaned forward and looked down, long-nailed, red-painted fingertips pressed to her temples. Blonde hair fell forward to hide her face. "First my name. I'm Sara, okay?"

"I'm Mike."

"Well Mike, my parents are very wealthy and very beautiful, so I'm what you would call a poor little rich girl. Too much pocket money, too much time, too much every-bloody-thing. There's a whole gang of us, a bunch of spoilt brats who while away the daylight hours riding, sailing and racing four-by-fours over our daddies' estates, then spend our nights getting pissed, stoned and screwing each other. A fulfilling and productive lifestyle, don't you think?"

Didn't sound too bad to me.

"This current little mess started when my *chum*—" the endearment was couched in bitter mockery "—Leanne found this ancient book in her Daddy's library. Pleasant little tome, all about black magic and witchcraft. She showed it to the gang and we decided to get together and raise a demon, just for a laugh. We said it would make a change from coke and fellatio."

She made it sound like a drink.

"So we drew our pentagram, chanted our chants, killed our chicken –

we were too stoned to worry about the blood – and giggled through the whole thing like the bunch of stupid bloody kids we were. Do you mind if I smoke?"

I didn't, so she lit up, hands shaking.

"It worked. It actually bloody worked. The room suddenly went cold and the French windows blew open. *That* scared us. But nothing else happened, not then." She dragged deeply at her cigarette and blew smoke in an elegant, disdainful manner that aroused me in the most alarming way.

"He came to me later that night, when I was in bed. I woke suddenly, and he was there. This gorgeous, huge, naked male. I wasn't frightened, just asked him who he was. 'I am Ash,' he said. 'You summoned me.'" She shuddered. "Then he fucked me. God, how he fucked me. He came back to me, night after night. Fucked and fucked and fucked me until it seemed that days were only meant for resting between fucks. Ash was all that mattered. All I ever thought about."

The November sun was now a bloody disk brooding over the horizon, staining the lower sky red and silhouetting trees and pylons. I noticed that the petrol was low.

"Then it got scary." Sara continued. "He began haunting me during the day. I saw his face in mirrors, reflected in shop windows, felt his breath on my neck. It was like being possessed."

Another deep drag.

"So last night, to break the spell I suppose, I went to a nightclub dressed like a tart, intending to seduce the first man who looked at me more than once. But Ash was there, naked and angry. No one else could see him. No matter how much I screamed and ranted and tried to make them. I remember being thrown out, but I can't remember finding my car, or getting into it. All I know is that I drove until I ran out of petrol, ran until I couldn't run anymore, then walked and walked and bloody walked. Christ I was scared. No one would give me a lift. No one would help me, Mike." She began to cry. "No one would fucking help me."

After a while, she wiped her eyes angrily with the back of her hand, then glanced over her shoulder. "Can't you go any faster? I think he's seen us."

My right foot slammed down. Stupid, but I couldn't help it. I was goose bumped, shivering. Her story and obvious distress were getting to me.

Hesitant, nervous of rejection, I reached for her hand. She grabbed at mine and held it tight. Her hand felt small, delicate, her palm sweat-damped. She was shaking.

"He's every-bloody-where Mike. I feel as if I'm going mad—" She sniffed loudly, then screamed.

The shock made me scream as well.

There, on the side of the dual carriageway, a man; dark, shoulder length, curly hair, Jason King moustache, naked.

Ash.

I knew it was him, just knew. For an instant, our eyes locked and he peeled away flesh, muscle, bone, laid open my soul, then whispered "wife killer" inside my head.

Then we were past him. I heard fear-moaning and realised it was me, in harmony with Sara's hysterical sobbing. My right foot was flat on the floor. The Astra estate's engine roared as if outraged at such treatment.

A glance in the mirror. He was chasing us. Dear God, *chasing* us. Running along the hard shoulder, taking huge, distorted strides. Like an image in a fish-eye lens, or a reflection in Satan's fairground mirror.

Couldn't think for Sara's wailing. I wanted her to shut up, shut up. "Shut up!"

She calmed slightly, looked behind. "You're losing him. Faster Mike. For God's sake faster."

"We need petrol."

"What? No, he'll catch us—"

"Look at the gauge Sara. Look at it. Look!"

"Oh God, oh Christ," she murmured, over and over. It sounded more like a prayer than blasphemy.

I glanced in the mirror again. Nothing but darkening dual carriageway and newly ignited head and tail lamps. Ahead, Rivenhall; petrol station, Little Chef, lights, cars, people, normality, sanctuary. I swung in and parked beside a pump.

"Hurry Mike. Please hurry."

No need to remind me. I was out, scrabbling at the lockable petrol cap, fumbling the nozzle into the aperture. The digital display counted the litres with torturous slowness. My hands shook, my eyes strayed across the forecourt, peering into the darkness beyond the island of electric light in which I hid.

Cars swept in and out. Engines stopped, idled, started. Doors opened, slammed. People talked, laughed. The warm glow spilling from the Little Chef brought on a coffee craving, reminded me that I was hungry, thirsty and tired. I hadn't stopped all day. One breakdown after another to investigate and repair. Desperate, stress-shredded office managers needing their photocopiers and fax machines working. Threatening that my bloody company would hear about it if I didn't get them back on line instantly with a wave of my magic screwdriver.

Still, it was a job, the first I'd managed to hold down since...

Ash.

Jogging onto the forecourt, naked. Horns blared, offence was shouted, someone even laughed. Which meant that this time he could be seen – meant he was real.

Our eyes locked again and his pace increased to a run. Those huge, distorted strides of his, eating the gap between us.

Almost upon me, barging a startled motorist aside, spilling wallet and coin across the concrete. I heard swearing, but saw only Ash, hands extended like claws – *were* claws. His eyes were white orbs. His mouth open, too wide, like the distended jaws of a hungry snake. Fangs instead of teeth. Flickering, forked tongue. He whispered "Wife killer," again and I sobbed, couldn't help it, couldn't stop.

Leaping now, wolf-like, roaring...

Instinct made me do it, made me swing the petrol pump nozzle round to spray petrol into Ash's face.

His roar became a howl of pain. He crashed to the ground at my feet, clawing at his eyes.

I reached behind myself and wrenched the car door open. Sara clawed and dragged at my clothes. I fell on to the driver's seat. Sara crawled over me, elbows, knees and heels poking and stabbing. For a moment, the barest instant, my terror was overwhelmed by perfume, woman smell, the erotic rustle of material over skin.

I glimpsed Ash getting to his feet, petrol-dripping, wavering. Saw Sara flick her lighted cigarette at him. Then there was blinding light, heat and agonised screeching.

Sara still across my lap, I struggled into a sitting position and managed to shove the key into the ignition. We careered away from the pumps, my door flapping open, people scattering before us. In the mirror, a burning figure lurched to its feet, stumbled after us. Not dead. Ash wasn't dead. Ash wasn't ash. I laughed, a slightly hysterical sound.

Onto the slip road. Sara wrestled herself back onto her seat. I slowed, just long enough to close my door. Then we were away, hurtling into darkness. Both gasping for breath, staring straight ahead, afraid to look in the mirror.

"Mike," Sara said, after a long pause. Her voice was soft, tremulous, all arrogance and bitch-edge gone.

"Yes?"

"Thank you." Her hand came to rest on my thigh. She sighed. I sensed some sort of struggle taking place, culminating in: "Perhaps you should dump me."

"I couldn't do that, Sara." Why not? I could drive away from this nightmare. The way I did before, leaving my dead behind. "Not to you."

The hand on my thigh tightened. "Mike, don't you understand? He'll never give up. He'll chase us forever."

"What's new?"

"Who are you?" Sara asked.

"I told you. Mike—"

"No. *Who?* Why are you helping me? Why didn't you throw me out when I started talking demons?"

I shrugged. She probably didn't see the gesture in the darkness. Anyway, she was busy lighting another cigarette.

"There are demons and there are demons," I said at last.

"What is that supposed to mean?"

"Creatures like Ash. And demons you can't see or fight."

"Such as?"

"Loneliness, guilt—"

"I'd be glad to swap."

"—and the good old psychiatric wing of your friendly local hospital."

"Oh, I see." She sounded embarrassed. Then: "Perhaps it's your turn to tell *me* about it."

"You don't want to know." Deja vu. We both laughed, a bitter sound.

"I do. Really." Our laughter softened. Hers seeped in to spread a warmth through me that I hadn't felt for a long time.

"My wife was killed in a car crash." Dear God, I'd managed to say it without breaking down. "I was driving." *Not your fault, Mike. Van parked too near the junction, you couldn't possibly have seen the other car as you pulled out. Was my fault though. I was driving so it was my fucking fault – steady, keep the door shut, keep it locked.*

"Christ Mike, I'm sorry."

Shaking. Wasn't going to give up though. Not now I'd started. "I drank at first. I thought that would shut the voices up."

"Voices?"

"In my head. My wife, God, Satan, demons, I don't know who the hell they were." Wife killer, they said. Wife killer. Wifekiller. Wifekiller WIFEKILLER—

I felt Sara's hand on my cheek. "Hey, Mike. It's all right. You don't have to tell me any more..."

"The booze didn't work. Neither did the psychiatrists or the drugs or the electric shock treatment. Oh, I made it look as if they did, but they didn't. Nothing worked. Except this."

"This?"

"Driving. It's why I've got this job – office equipment maintenance. Spending most my days alone, stuck behind the wheel of a car. A kind of penitence, I suppose. Forcing myself to relive the accident over and over again." I chuckled, an unhealthy sound. "So you see Sara, I'm on the run from demons as well. No one understands, no one can help. No one even wants to."

"I do," Sara said, so quietly I could barely hear her.

Sign board, green-glowing and disembodied in our headlights. Seven miles to the M25. I was disappointed. I wanted the journey to last forever...

Ash was on the bonnet.

Crouching, cat-like. Fire-ruined face twisted into a feral snarl, rags of charred flesh flapping in the slipstream. He glowed, as if still burning. I was screaming, or perhaps it was Sara, or both of us. Didn't know. Couldn't tell.

He touched the windscreen. Pushed a taloned hand through the glass as though it was water. Reaching for my face, my eyes. I was driving blind, right foot slammed flat onto the floor. Too fast. A car horn blared somewhere outside. Angry, yet distant. I was frozen, transfixed by Ash's sharp, sharp claw...

Sara wrenched the steering wheel from my grip. The car swerved left. Ash fell backwards, almost toppled onto the road, ripped his hand back through the windscreen to claw and scrabble at the smooth surface of the bonnet. I saw the hard shoulder, trees, hedges, closing in on my left. I twisted the wheel to the right. Something burst from my blind spot. Another horn blared.

Left again. Nearside wheels juddering along the bank, branches raking the bonnet, pummelling the windscreen.

Ash disappeared.

Back onto the carriageway. Still flat out. Still yelling and screaming.

Sara's screams became words: "We have to stop."

"No. No. Mustn't stop. We've lost him. He's gone—"

"We have to stop, you stupid bastard!"

I was stung into silence.

She calmed down, softened. "I'm sorry Mike, but we need a place, a room, so we can face him down, get rid of him. There are rituals. I copied them out of Leanne's book." She produced a crumpled piece of A4 from her coat pocket. "I could have tried before, but I'm too frightened to do this on my own." A pause. "And it might make things worse."

"How much worse?"

"Other... things have to be summoned to take Ash back."

"Demons on demons," I muttered, then took a deep breath to calm myself. "Okay, okay. We'll stop."

Her hand returned to my thigh. "I'll pay you back for this, Mike. Whatever you want."

"Just stay with me, Sara."

She leaned across to kiss me.

We booked into the Brentwood Post House, nestled in the traffic-noisy armpit of the A12/M25 junction. Our room was pleasantly square, clean and anonymous.

I slumped gratefully onto the bed. Sara thrust a heavy marker pen into my hand. "Draw a pentagram. On the floor, in front of the door."

"What?" Uncomprehending, confused.

"Christ, don't you know anything?" Fear was sharpening her tongue. "A five-pointed star. Make it big enough for a person to stand in. And hurry, for God's sake."

I dropped to my knees and began scrawling a star on the light fawn, short-piled carpet. Vaguely I wondered what the cleaner would make of it in the morning. Then I wondered if there would be a morning. My gut squirmed, the shaking grew worse. We were trapped in here. If this didn't work, there would be nothing but claws and teeth. And those eyes, slowly ripping my soul apart...

Sara was reading from the sheet of paper she had shown me, muttering to herself; dark, bad words that were nonetheless strangely comforting. *Dear God, let her get this right.*

"Finished." I struggled to my feet.

"Blood," Sara muttered. "Need something sharp."

I produced a penknife from my jacket pocket and cracked the good Boy Scout joke.

She smiled weakly, took the knife from my hand, then stepped across to the pentagram and with a sudden, decisive movement, sliced the blade across her left palm. Blood spattered onto the carpet.

She spoke: "Darkest of Dark. Lightest of Light, come unto me. Lucifer Bright-Angel, Prince of the Powers of the air, come unto me. Lord of Lies—"

The lights flickered, dimmed. The temperature dropped, I shivered uncontrollably. There was a smell of rotting meat. Though the window was tight-shut, the curtains stirred and rustled. The glossy hotel pamphlets on the bedside table flapped open and blew onto the floor.

Sara stood before the pentagram, body rigid. "Morning Star," she murmured and dropped the knife. I found myself going to her, holding her bleeding hand. It was trembling, slippery-hot.

I heard whisperings. "Doors are opening little butterfly. Doors on doors."

A glass smashed in the bathroom. We both flinched, hand crushing hand. The television blared into life, channel-skipping itself in a stroboscopic madness of blare and crackle, blare and crackle. The bedside phone rang. A light bulb exploded – a sudden rain of sparks and glass.

Then silence, just as sudden, just as shocking.

Something came into the room. A shadow, glimpsed from the corner of the eye, an indistinct foulness staining the air. So oppressive, so cold and absolutely malevolent that it made me cry. I couldn't help it. I was frightened and filled with unutterable despair and loneliness and grief.

It spoke, a wet-breathed growl. "What do you want?" The sound of it brought a fresh wave of weeping. Each syllable drove fiery pain into my joints, weakening my legs, vice-crushing my arms and neck.

"Take Ash back to yourself." Sara's voice was barely audible.

"Are you sure?"

"Yes...Please...Please..." Sara almost broke then. I wanted to hold her, but couldn't move.

"Doors on doors on doors..." it persisted. I saw them; dark doors, slamming open, letting things through. Awful things.

Footsteps, outside, Ash was coming.

"Take him away. Please take him...please..."

The footsteps grew louder, slowed, stopped. *In the name of God, hurry up, don't let him in here...*

"He loves you, Sara."

"I don't care."

And the door burst open. Ash. Beautiful again. The perfection of him more terrible than his fire-ruin. I tried to avert my eyes from his, but his stare tore them back. He was in my skull again, chanting his now familiar litany, the acid lickings of that silent voice almost an old friend; wifekiller...wifekiller...

"Look at him, little butterfly. Look at what you could have." The growl of that other thing became persuasive, honey-dipped, not unpleasant. "Don't you want him?"

"No…Yes…" She was giving in. Dear God, giving in.

"Sara," I whispered. "Don't—"

"DO NOT INTERFERE, MICHAEL WIFEKILLER." The force of it slammed me backwards and crushed me against the bed. My bladder let go. I tasted blood – nosebleed.

Godlike, Ash towered over Sara, filling the open doorway, gently touching her face, whispering her name. I saw her shiver, heard her soft moans.

"Take…Ash…away." Sara's voice was a groan of effort. "Please take him. Please…"

"As you wish, Sara." It sounded like genuine regret. "The choice is yours."

Ash recoiled; there was hurt on his face. Then rage.

The illusion shattered. And Ash was a ruin of raw, fire-blistered flesh hanging in tatters from red-glistening muscle and white-gleaming bone. The grey-white smoothness of his skull showed through a charred hole in his scalp. Blood and other ichors dripped from him. The stench of burned flesh slithered into my nostrils, churned my gut.

He roared, lurched towards us, stepped into the pentagram.

And was gone.

Air popped into the vacuum. Then nothing.

Sara stumbled backwards. I scrambled across the floor to catch her as she fell. She felt frail and small in my arms. We huddled together, both of us trembling, sobbing. Ash was gone. The other was gone.

But something else was out there, coming our way. I could feel it. A long way off, but coming.

Sara sobbed then stirred in my arms. Her lips sought mine. Her breath was hot; I tasted tear-salt in my mouth. As I pushed her down onto the floor, let her pull me urgently down on top of her, I saw her eyes. Hell eyes. Wild with the terror of what we had done, of what would come upon her. Upon *us*.

Doors had been opened…

No matter Sara. I'll stay with you, because your demons are mine now and my demons are yours.

FRACTURE

This would be the fourth time the Fracture's solar orbit took it through the narrow stretch of space between Earth and its moon.

Probes had been sent, of course, and data collected, but the exact nature of the apparently mass-less and gravity-free phenomenon remained elusive.

The Fracture was a wonder and a terror, because its six-day dominance of the sky tore away the fragile veneer of rationality humankind had formed over its innate fear of heaven-sent destruction. And because once the hysteria and killings ceased with the end of the Fracture's first visit, rumour, eye-witness account then scientific hypothesis agreed that a significant proportion of the world's populace had been affected. They had, it was whispered-reported-stated, been turned into rabid beasts, had become werewolves in all but fur and fang, Fracture-crazed lycanthromorphs, lykes...

1

A snatch of autumn gusted into the Close to trouble scraps of rubbish escaped from cat-torn, uncollected refuse bags. The sky was cloud-grey and sunless and, to the west, discoloured by streaks of red that resembled lines of poison spreading along the flesh of an infected limb.

Four doors from where Richard Evans nailed plywood sheets over the windows of his three-bed semi, a neighbour hurried panic-bought shopping from car to house.

She knows I'm here, Richard Evans mused from atop his ladder, *but she won't speak, won't even glance in my direction.* Too near Fracture Rise for neighbours to risk communicating with a lyke, not that anyone attempted conversation with him at all anymore.

There had been other lykes in the Close, all of them named and shamed by the tabloids and decently moved away. Not Richard. He had already lost his college lecturer post and he was not about to let anyone drive him out of his own home.

Because he *wasn't* a lyke.

Rather, he was a victim of hearsay, innuendo and smear, the judge, jury and executioner in these paranoid times.

The neighbour's front door slammed shut.

The Close was once more empty.

Bearing down on his anger, Richard returned his attention to the job in hand, pushing a sheet of plywood over the window of the spare bedroom with one hand and nail-gunning it in place with the other. Sweat dripped into his eyes.

They hunt in packs you see, and eat human flesh...

Work done, Richard turned to gaze at the red stain in the sky. Eight hours to Fracture Rise.

He climbed down the ladder. Time to go indoors and pack his suitcase ready for his six-day confinement as all lykes, good, true and presumed were now legally obliged to do. He would be gone before Louise arrived home from work, but she would be safe. No lyke would get into *his* house and hurt *his* wife.

Not that he had ever actually seen a lyke...

2

There was a tabloid on Headmaster Nicholas Reynolds' desk.

"Sit down Louise," he said breezily, then offered a smile, startling in its insincerity.

Louise Evans perched herself on a chair. The office was quiet, neat, well organised.

"I'm afraid that we have a difficulty."

Louise didn't answer. Let him squirm.

Reynolds picked up the newspaper, opened it at "Today's Lyke List" then turned it about so that Louise could see the faces and names. His carefully manicured forefinger came to rest on one particular portrait.

"Is that your husband?"

Louise managed a dry-voiced "Yes."

"Why didn't you tell us?"

Louise didn't answer, was transfixed instead by Richard's grainy face with its neat beard and frame of too long hair. The camera had caught him glancing back over his shoulder in mid-stride. Perhaps he had seen the camera flash, sensed that someone had snapped him surreptitiously as he crossed the Close. It *was* the Close; Louise recognised some of the houses in the background. Houses that belonged to people she had known for almost ten years – friends, or so she thought.

There was money to be made from such photography.

"Richard is not a lyke."

"You have to face up to this."

"Face up to what, for God's sake? Richard had to hide during the last Fracture Rise, not to stop him hunting human flesh but to keep *him* safe from our own bloody neighbours."

"We have a Duty of Care towards the children here."

"You're not listening, are you?"

"Louise, parents will see this photograph and…Houses have been burned, lykes and their families dragged out into the street and beaten."

"And you're afraid they'll tear down the school just because one of the teachers is the wife of an alleged, an *alleged*, lyke?" She wanted to scream and slap Reynolds' face.

"The bottom line is that we want you to resign. You'll be given a good package but we can no longer afford the risk. You are not the only staff member in this situation. Believe me, if I had a choice—"

She didn't hear the rest, blotted it out with a slammed door.

Outside the air was smoke-flavoured; something burned beyond the playground's ten foot plate-steel and razor-wire fence. Glass broke, there were shouts. A siren blasted past the school.

Louise made it to the car dry-eyed, slumped into the driver's seat and let it come. She sobbed, gagged, screamed and hammered the palms of her hands against the steering wheel rim. Then she covered her face and rocked and wept until she was done.

Exhausted, she looked up to see that the afternoon gloom had descended a notch towards twilight. The classroom lights glowed warmly.

Louise started the engine—

Go on, straight into the school doors.

—put the Toyota into first and made the tight arc towards the main gates.

The barrier rose and the security guard waved her out, no doubt already aware of her status, car registration noted so that she would never be allowed back in.

Never.

She tried to comprehend what had just happened, how her meaning, her purpose had suddenly been torn out of her—

A vehicle tore across the junction ahead; lorry, army-green, followed by another, then a Land Rover, aerial waving.

The street ran through a residential area, Council Houses mostly, with neglected front gardens. A lot of people were gathered by their fences, at their gates and on the pavements, talking, staring, pointing.

Smoke boiled up from beyond the rooftops to Louise's right.

Blue flashing light hurtled towards her then past, fire engine. Its backwash rocked the Toyota. Louise glimpsed raised fists and middle-fingers from the crowd.

Suddenly people were spewed from the side streets to her right, running from the smoke, momentarily surrounding the car. The waiting residents cheered them, welcomed them back with hugs and high-fives.

Job done, lykes burned.

And was that such a bad thing? Weren't they the cause of all this heartache and bloodshed? Didn't the good of the many far outweigh the health of the few?

She pulled away and braked again; soldiers this time, carrying guns. *Oh God, guns!*

One of them swung round, hand raised, silhouetted by the gloom then painted by her headlamps. She stopped.

I'm a teacher, not a criminal. I'm with you...

The soldier tapped on her window. He was young, grim-faced, afraid even.

"Where are you going?"

"Home, out of town."

"Where've you been?"

"At work."

I used to teach.

More soldiers joined him, alert, nervous. They asked Louise to get out of the car, to raise her hands. A torch was shone in her face. She was made to lean on the bonnet, hands splayed on the warm metal. She tried to think, to breathe. There was a woman's voice, stern, abrupt, then hands under her arms, down her sides, feeling and touching, invading the ultimate private space that was her body.

"She's clear," the woman said.

"Car's clear."

"Sorry love," the young soldier said. "Drive safely. Get yourself home and lock your doors."

If she had had the strength Louise would have cried again but she was too hollow, exhausted and humiliated, so utterly humiliated.

Once out of the town, she saw that other glow, flickering from below the horizon, reaching up to taint the sky's black purity.

3

Richard Evans closed his suitcase and leaned on its dark blue lid, fingers spread, arms locked.

They were going to shut him away, lock him in, bury him...

It was well organised. A coach, escorted by a truck full of soldiers and a Land Rover, would stop at the war memorial. There would be police, a list.

And broken down front doors at the houses of the absent.

Better to volunteer, to come quietly, even if you weren't actually a lyke. It was only for six days then all would be normal again and he could return home. To live amongst the neighbours who believed him to be a monster, who had whispered rumours into the wrong ears.

Last Fracture Rise he had fled to a cheap, no-questions-asked hotel in London, to protect Louise, to save his own home and hearth. This time there was an official letter, a demand that he report for temporary confinement, in an ex-holiday camp of all places, now barb-wired and watch-tower guarded.

Six days, promised on television, on radio, from the lips of Cabinet Ministers and Police Commissioners. As always, the UK was ahead of the rest of the world in its handling of the crisis and showing the right mix of compassion and firmness.

But confinement was confinement, a cage was a cage...

He should go, now.

So he didn't miss the coach, so his front door, armoured, extra-locked and lyke-proof, wasn't broken down by a police battering ram.

A car.

He paused, the case half lifted from the duvet. The engine grew loud then stopped. A door slammed. The front door opened. Louise then, but far too early.

She would call out to him. She always called.

Haven't you gone yet Richard? Are you okay?

She had come home to see him off, to hold him one last time before...

But there was no shout, just footsteps, the cupboard, a clink of bottle and glass.

Grabbing the case, Richard hurried downstairs. He found Louise in the lounge. She was on the sofa, shoes on – normally the first thing kicked off – coat buttoned, eyes hard.

"You're early," Richard said. The words were redundant.

Louise sipped Southern Comfort and lemonade, her favourite.

"It's only for six days." Another useless, much worn fact.

"No it isn't." She wouldn't look at him. "It's not just six days is it, or six bloody months."

"Louise, what are you talking about?"

"You're a lyke, Richard. Once a lyke, always a lyke."

How he hated that cliché, coined by the media and now the currency of the masses.

"I lost my job today."

"What?"

"They sacked me because I'm married to a lyke." Another swig. "I'm a school teacher, I teach little kids and they love me and they are not afraid of me. Some of my pupils are lykes but I don't see them anymore because it's too dangerous to have them around, even after the Fracture sets and they're the same as the rest of us again. They don't even live in the town anymore because the non-lykes, the *normal* folk, broke their windows and daubed shit on their doors."

There was, of course, no answer or action Richard could take because Louise was clenched into herself so tightly there was no possibility of holding, or even touching, her.

"It's your fault," she said suddenly. "It's your fault, Richard. You did this to me. You!"

He shook his head. No, it was the Fracture, freak of nature, a cosmic phenomenon that led to the rumours, innuendo and accusation.

"Go away." Louise was ominously calm. "And don't ever come back."

He took a step towards her, a mistake because it splintered her drink-strengthened self-control.

"*I don't want you anymore!*" She screamed then gasped for breath, surged to her feet, held herself tightly and faced the wall and when Richard put his hands on her arms, she spun round and smashed the glass in his face.

Sometime later Richard found himself outside with no suitcase or coat and only the clothes he stood up in. He made to go back into the house but stopped. The coach was coming; if he didn't show up the police would come and then it would become terrible. But he couldn't leave her...

Christ, what should he do?

He tasted blood and its warm, salty flavour made him sick.

There would be medical help at the camp. Someone would have a First Aid box, wouldn't they? He had to go, to protect Louise.

He walked from the house, cold now in the sharp October evening air.

Six days, six days, six days...

He stopped and looked up at the horizon of rooftops to his right. The sky pulsed red, great loops of energy rose, arced and burst. The beauty of it transfixed him. Not long now.

You couldn't see the Fracture from inside a cell. There were, it was reported, no windows.

Only walls and a door that was no longer a door because doors were designed to be opened as well as closed.

He tasted blood and resumed his walk towards the war memorial.

Where there were police cars, lights a-flash and radios a-crackle, and a small crowd – quiet for now – faces appearing-vanishing-appearing in the blue-light stroboscope. Someone shouted as Richard approached. They would be shocked, perhaps pleased by the blood on his face and shirt.

A constable cut off his progress.

"I'm sorry sir you can't..." His eyes widened. "Are you okay?"

"I'm here for the coach."

The sympathy drained from the constable's eyes and voice, which he raised to a shout. "I need some help here." What for exactly? To assist with an injured man or because he was confronted with a flesh-eating, Fracture-maddened lyke?

A WPC crossed with a business-like efficiency that could not hide an eagerness for skull-cracking. Her right hand went to the grip of her truncheon or riot stick or whatever those modern complications of cross-piece and moulded handles were called these days.

"What happened to you?"

Do I care? Whoever started it should have finished it...

"An accident..."

"You'd better come with me. I've a first aid kit in the car."

More shouts from the crowd, jeering. "Let him bleed."

"All right, that's enough." A half-hearted order from the first constable.

Richard crouched down beside the car while the WPC dabbed at his face. He flinched as chemicals stung open wounds. "You need some stitches in this," she said. "I'll stick some steri-strips over the worst of them. There's a doctor at the camp, he'll sort you out properly." She sounded tender now, as if some humanitarian instinct had overridden her distaste for lykes.

"I'm not a lyke," Richard said as the dressings were applied then wished he hadn't because it sounded pathetic. The WPC's reply was an order. "Okay, wait over there by the memorial with the others."

The others turned out to be a teenage girl, a frail-looking old man, dapper in his heavy coat and trilby, and an equally frail lady who looked to be his wife and clutched tenaciously at his arm. The girl leaned on the memorial itself, hands in the pockets of her jeans. The old man nodded uncertainly to Richard.

"I don't understand," he began, voice tremulous. "I'm not a...you know. And neither is my wife, but they seem to think she is. There's been a dreadful mistake. I couldn't let her go on her own. Perhaps someone will listen at the camp."

The woman said nothing, just stared and Richard saw then how terribly blank that stare was. Richard wanted to offer some reassurance but could only shrug and hope the gesture sympathetic.

This group then, represented the three remaining lykes of Abbotsfield, the village's fearsome hunters of the Fracture-stained night.

Richard stamped feeling into his feet and tried to rub it into his tee-shirt-bare arms. His teeth clattered. The teenage girl slipped down the rough, martyr-carved stone to sit on the monument's concrete step. The old man muttered platitudes to his shivering, blank-eyed wife. It was going to be all right, he would explain everything when they got to the camp and they'd be home in the warm in no time.

The crowd watched and coughed and murmured. There were snatches of laughter, the occasional shouted insult.

Engine noise rattled into earshot then headlights, several pairs, swept round the corner to wash over the war memorial and its visitors. First a Land Rover jerked to a halt, then a lorry. Soldiers emerged, their movements quick and malevolently efficient. There were guns, helmets. Finally the main transport arrived, white and green with "Carter's Coaches" printed jauntily on the side. Doors hissed open.

The teenager unfolded herself and sauntered towards the vehicle. She paused to let the elderly couple on first then glanced back at Richard and he saw absolute terror on her gaunt, multi-pierced face. Tears streaked her zombie mascara. Richard followed her into the coach and heard the doors hiss shut behind him.

4

The coach was full, its passengers mostly silent. The teenage girl sat next to Richard as if seeking some sort of security in his presence. The elderly couple were on the opposite side of the aisle, the old man long since given up trying to reassure his wife and now staring ahead, face made sickly by the subdued lighting.

There were two guards, bored-looking soldiers who sat in the front seats. The anonymous driver was sealed into a makeshift, armoured cab. No guided tour this.

The engine drone was soporific. Richard's face stung, his head ached. Blood still seeped into his mouth. Some of the adhesive strips put in place by the WPC had peeled away allowing the cuts to re-open. His eyes grew heavy...

Sudden hard braking threw Richard forward then flung him back into the seat. Someone cried out. He saw the elderly man clutching at his forehead, face creased with pain.

Then one of the windows, further towards the front, exploded inwards.

A moment later there was a bright flash and a wave of heat.

It took a moment to comprehend. Fire; someone had stopped the coach and thrown a firebomb through the window. People were screaming. Christ, *burning*...

He shoved at the teenage girl who seemed paralysed. He shouted at her, his voice lost in the shrieks of agony and panic. The girl started and scrambled out into the aisle.

A second firebomb crashed into the coach, this one from the opposite side.

Richard saw the girl join the struggle for the rear window then he grabbed at the old man's arm, bony through the sleeve of his coat. The man, in turn, clung to his wife. He wouldn't move, wouldn't come. Bodies collided with Richard, beat at him. The coach was filling with smoke, shuddering under the impact of fists and boots that hammered at its flanks from outside.

A third firebomb. Richard saw it clearly; a bottle, flame spewing from its cloth-stuffed neck. Then he was pushed forward onto the floor by the fresh wave of heat. Bodies piled on top of him and, in a panic of animal claustrophobia, Richard punched and bit and clawed his way to the surface. People were heaped over the rear seat, screaming and fighting as flame bore down on them.

Fists beat at the rear window.

Then someone got it open and poured himself through. Others brawled their way into the space. Coughing, gagging, on his knees, Richard saw hands reach in to drag the passengers out.

Murdering hands...

The girl was crouched on the floor next to him. She made to scramble onto the back seat. Richard grabbed her leg and yanked her down again.

The heat seared his flesh, his throat. Every breath was agony.

But he waited, arms around the girl, as near to the floor as possible, trying to stay beneath the smoke.

The rush eased, the shouts and screams had moved to the outside. He uncurled himself and crawled along the hot floor, to the seat. Up, carefully, aware that the girl was behind him.

Onto the seat now, a glance back, flame, odd, black shapes in some of the seats and on the floor, human-like but far from human anymore. Cautiously he raised himself until he could see out of the rear window.

He saw the road, high hedges. He saw what looked like bundles strewn over the tarmac, visible in the fire-glow, their dancing shadows giving them an erratic half-life. He saw others, standing, staring. A woman smoked a cigarette, another held a child's hand and pointed at the coach in the way a mother points at a bonfire on November 5th, a man cracked open a can. They all carried weapons; clubs, spades, knives. Their faces and clothes were blood-splashed. The group, four or five of them, talked and laughed then strolled towards the coach. They disappeared along its offside.

The girl coughed and gagged; Richard grabbed her hand and hauled her up to the open window. Then they were out where it was cold, blood-slicked and terrible.

Dragging the girl, Richard ran along the side of the road, searching the hedgerow for a gateway, a gap, anything.

Voices.

A shout.

He scrambled onto the verge and rammed himself into the hedge. It clawed, scratched and tore. But he was through, slithering downwards into the tangled undergrowth and icy mud of a ditch that bordered a ploughed field. The girl was still with him, her breath ragged sobs.

Richard offered the girl his hands and she clambered out. He followed with much clawing and struggling. When he finally straightened up and drew in fresh cold air he saw that the Fracture was rising.

5

Answer, for God's sake Richard, answer your bloody phone...

Louise paced, cordless clamped against her ear, left arm tight about herself, shoes and coat still securely in place. On and on it rang. Then came the phone company's answering service; "...leave a message..."

She had already left a message, a hundred messages. So she dialled again, and again and again.

Please God, Christ, any one, make my husband answer his phone.

They were out there, the lykes. She could hear them, running, darting, scuttling about the Close, moving in on the house. Hungry...

There, voices, echoing through the still autumn air.

"Die," she shouted at them through the boarded-up windows. "Why don't you die?"

Another sound, a siren, then slammed doors and footsteps. Someone shouted, voice amplified by a megaphone, at her, shouted at *her*. A weight slammed into the front door. Another and another.

She collapsed onto her knees, shaking and sobbing.

I want my husband, she cried, all tears and snot. I want Richard...

A crash, more shouts. In the house now; the lykes were in the house. She crawled across the floor, trying to hide, behind the sofa, anywhere. The shouting was terrible. Figures erupted into the lounge, she glimpsed them and screamed. Hands had her, pushing her down onto the floor.

"Police! Don't move. *Don't move.*"

The house was filled with boot steps, with crashing and breaking and tearing. Louise felt her arms wrenched behind her.

Someone shouted. "Not here sarge!"

"Where is he?" Yelled into her ear. She felt cuffs clicked into place. She couldn't move. "Where's the lyke bastard you screw with? Huh? Come on, tell me!"

"Guh...Gone..." The word was choked out. She couldn't think, too many people and voices, too much violence and pain. "Con...confine...."

"Liar. He's on the run. He's come back here, hasn't he. *Hasn't he.*"

"No..."

"Lying lyke-whore."

"I...I'm n...nuh...not..."

"Perhaps you're lying about what *you* are."

She didn't know what he meant. She wanted to move her contorted, agonised arms, to turn her head and breathe.

"No decent woman would screw a lyke, would they? *Would they?*"

She couldn't answer, she didn't *know* the answer.

"Maybe you'd like to come out and howl at the Fracture."

They hauled her to her feet and she collapsed so they had to drag her outside, stumbling, almost falling. There was a car. Its dazzling blue light confused her. People were gathered outside her house; she could hear their shocked, excited gabble.

The police bundled her into the road then spun her about to face the vast bloodstain spreading across the sky.

"Here it comes," the sergeant shouted. People cheered.

A red line formed at the point where rooftops met the sky. The line thickened into a dome from which arcs of energy strained outwards and burst. The dome swelled until it became the leading edge of an immense red disk. The disk's surface was veined with streaks of energy. Fire writhed and boiled on its surface.

And it rumbled – the sound, many said, of its pulse.

The thing climbed swiftly skywards; a vast, bloody heart, a scarlet eye, a huge suppurating wound.

The sound thudded through the air, through the earth, through

Louise's skull and twisted her own heartbeat into synch with its own.

The Fracture.

"Feels good does it?" the sergeant, her tormentor, yelled. She had forgotten that he was holding her arm. "Want to howl do you?" He laughed then looked round at the crowd of neighbours. "What are you lot looking at? Get on with it."

No...Louise tried to shout but there was no energy or words left.

People ran toward her house. They carried petrol cans, milk and wine bottles all filled with fluids they were definitely not intended for.

They must have had those things ready... God, her neighbours, her friends, now cheering, whooping and laughing as the first Molotov cocktail arced towards her open front door.

Someone shouted. *Burn the lyke as well...*

The shout became a chant.

The police looked on.

6

A shot.

Christ, *a shot*. Someone was actually trying to shoot him. The reality of it almost drove Richard to his knees.

But he ran on, shambling over ploughed earth because to stop would mean death.

Thank God for the Fracture's glare, for the distorted shadows it threw, and for the distance he and the teenage girl had covered before one of the escorting soldiers had seen fit to check out if anyone had escaped from either the burning coach or the lynch mob.

The soldiers had let it happen... Richard recalled no shooting, no voices raised in prohibition. *They must have stood by and watched, taken part even...*

On and on then, towards the wood which lay on the far side of the field, the sobbing, gagging girl in tow, hoping that his pursuers were as hampered by the field's ridges and dips as he was. The Fracture dominated the sky beyond the trees. Its blood-stain filled every crevice. It shifted and boiled and its thrumming pulse pounded at the earth.

What about Louise?

Safe, had to be; he had boarded up the windows. She wasn't a lyke, no one would hurt her. Would they?

Would they...

Richard glimpsed figures breasting then paralleling him like the jaws of a trap. None were uniformed, the army escort content to let the civvies do their dirty work. The pursuers carried iron bars and spades and other blunt objects.

He could hear their breathing now, their muttered curses. He felt his legs weakening. Not long now. So why fight and delay the inevitable? A few moments of pain then it would be over, no more persecution and hiding and fear. At least Louise was safe. That was all that mattered now.

Moments of pain?

Those bastards wanted to *beat* them both to death, to pummel and maim and destroy. How many blows would it take? How many agonising connections of iron and wood with flesh?

He became aware of the girl's hand crushed in his own. He couldn't let them smash her to pieces.

Don't stop... don't bloody stop...

But he had to, because he could not run any longer...

He glanced round again and saw that, unbelievably, their pursuers had fallen back, had faded into anonymous, Fracture-distorted shapes. They were only ordinary people after all; smokers, drinkers, the fast-food bloated, their killing lust losing out to the raw survival-need that energised Richard's limbs and heart far beyond their normal measure.

Richard didn't slow, despite the pleading of the girl, whose voice was found at last. Had to keep going, stumbling, tripping, falling, crashing over the frozen soil.

There was a wood, within reach, God, actually within reach! Richard hauled air into his burning lungs, forced his legs to move, to work.

"Almost there, almost there..." A gasped litany.

Then they were.

Hidden now, they limped on through the black-then-red chaos of the Fracture-painted trees. He heard shouts, distant now, but *there*. The hunters were still blood-hungry, recovering their collective breath, reforming.

A hundred yards later Richard and the girl found an abandoned farm.

7

A snatch of autumn gusted into the farmyard to trouble leaves and scraps of rubbish. Only half the sky was night-black, the rest glowed red and boiled and pulsed like a heart that bled fire. Below the ladder on which Richard Evans was perched, the teenage girl dumped a sheet of corrugated steel onto the growing pile of scavenged materials that included a reel of barbed wire and several sharpened fence posts.

There were tools in the barns, food in the farmhouse, all giving the impression of sudden, Mary Celeste desertion. Whether through fear or persecution, Richard couldn't tell.

He returned his attention to the job in hand, pushing a sheet of plywood over a bedroom window with one hand and hammering it in place with the other. Sweat dripped into his eyes. He was hot, feverishly so.

The hammer thumped and bucked in his hand. Got to use enough nails, got to make it secure.

Because they hunt in packs you see...

THERE IS A WAY TO LIVE FOREVER

(Based on an idea by Jessica Lawrence)

Our special place.

The early morning sky bleeds cold drizzle as we walk through the dank woods. The path, wet and slippery, runs between the trees and the river. She holds my hand, hers warm and trembling, mine cold. I walk slowly, so as not to drag her along, because she can't walk fast.

It is high tide, the current strong as the three-mile distant North Sea forces its way upstream. The river is wide too and vast and cold.

My body functions, despite the deadness of its nervous system. Most of my mind has shut down. The remaining part simply calculates, when and how...

The path narrows.

I grip her hand more tightly. She protests. I stop, turn, tell her I'm sorry. I frame the words precisely; modulate my voice so the word doesn't come out as a sob. She frowns, not understanding.

I look at the river, at the steepness of the bank, black-green water surges by, its coldness palpable.

I hold her arms.

"I love you," I sob.

And wrench her round and hurl her over the bank into the icy, fast-flowing water. Scream and splash mingle. Her bright blue coat tears a momentary gash into the river's turbulent patterning.

Then she's gone...

"I know you."

"I don't think so." I'm gasping for a cigarette. No smoking in here though, not in Alan and Kat's vast and shinily appointed kitchen.

The woman stares at me. Tongue-tied, I smile back and shrug. I should say something but no witticism is forthcoming. It's been a long time since I made small talk with an attractive woman. Other than my wife, of course, but that doesn't count, does it?

"It's so weird." The woman is in her thirties, the early ones if the party-dim lighting isn't being over-kind. "I'm sure I've seen you before." She holds out her hand. "I'm Miriam," she says.

I take the hand and the flesh-on-flesh contact snatches my breath.

The opening chords of "Brown Sugar" saw from the lounge-now-dance-floor, people cheer. All of us, Alan and Kat's party guests, are of a certain age, too young to have been interested when the Stones recorded the song, but old enough for it to be skewered into our collective consciousness.

"Rob," I say and her eyes widen as if in surprise. They are dark as her long, lush hair.

"Oh, so *you're* Rob."

What?

"Kat told me about you. God, it must be hard."

If it wasn't for those eyes, that hair and the soft jumper that bares her shoulders by clinging precariously, as if by some woollen magic, to her upper arms, I would have made my excuses.

I shrug instead.

"I mean, bringing up your daughter on your own after..." Her hand goes to her mouth. "Oh God, I'm so sorry. Look, it's none of my business..."

"It's okay," I shout above Mick and Keith. It isn't. It will never be okay. "Come on, I'll get you a drink Miriam." I like the taste of her name.

Her smile is apologetic and uncertain this time. We push our way to the drinks table. I ask her what she wants and move close to hear her answer. The perfumed heat of her proximity gives me an erection so hard it hurts.

"Fruit juice...driving," she yells and our eyes catch. My mouth dries and she bites at her lower lip. Suddenly breathing is harder than it was a moment ago.

Christ, how long is it since anything like this has happened to me? How many years, decades?

"Are you Jewish?" I ask a little later, when we are sitting on the stairs, like teenagers. Her arm is tight against mine. We pretend not to notice.

She laughs. "Does it matter?"

"Of course not. The name's the clue. Miriam is the Virgin Mary's real name."

"It isn't the big hooked nose?"

"Well, that as well."

"So, what is Rob another name for?" she says.

I have never thought about it before. Rob is just...Rob.

"Robert." *I suppose.*

From the lounge, as if on cue, my apparent namesake slides into the lyrics of "Stairway to Heaven" and without a further word I stand, hold out my hand and drown in hair, soft wool and the taste of those creamy, bare shoulders.

After the party, I sit in Miriam's Citroën, parked by the pavement a few yards from my two-bedroom terrace. She has brought me home because I'm over the limit. I'll pick my own car up from Alan and Kat's tomorrow.

Suddenly awkward, we stare ahead through the rapidly steaming windscreen.

"I'd...I'd love to invite you in but...Anna ...she's only six. If she wakes up..."

"I understand. It's okay." Miriam is a heavy-coated, sweet-scented shadow.

I reach for her hand. "I'd like to see you again," The sentence feels stilted, messy.

"So would I." Soft, almost a whisper.

Another moment. Then I lean across and she meets me halfway and we kiss, clumsy across the handbrake.

So now I'm in love and it is as adolescent and blinding and foolish as it used to be.

"Anna was a bit fretful after you went, Rob," Janet Fenning calls out as I hang my coat in the hall. "She must've cried for an hour, poor little mite."

Janet, neighbour and babysitter, emerges from the kitchen. She is a large, wheezing woman with an unruly mop of grey hair. "Don't look so worried," she says. "She's bound to play up a bit. This must be the first time you've gone out since you moved here."

Since Chrissie's death, as a matter of fact.

"Is she asleep now?"

"I think so. I've read her enough stories to last her a lifetime." Janet chuckles. "Mog the Cat! I was glad when the stupid animal finally popped her clogs—" Again that look of horror. "Oh I am sorry Rob. That was stupid of me..."

"It's okay, really it is."

And tonight, for the first time in six years, it is.

"Would you like me to make you a coffee or anything?" Janet is long-deserted and lonely.

Yes, so I can sit and tell you all about Miriam, like the lovesick teenager I've become.

"No thanks, I think I'll get straight to bed."

Anna cries out the moment Janet shuts the front door. I look up to see her on the landing.

"I had a bad dream."

I sweep her up into my arms. "Come on, I'll read you a story."

"I don't like you going away."

"I wasn't away."

"You were."

"Only for a little while." Anna has blonde hair. Her face is Nordic, serious, Chrissie's hair and face, naturally.

Hardly the right word for it, *naturally*.

"I dreamed we were going to the shops and then you let go of my hand and ran away and I cried but you wouldn't come back." There is a fraught edge to her voice that makes my flesh crawl.

"It was just a dream," I say as I take her back to her bedroom.

Tonight, Miriam wears a little black dress. She's no waif, she has shape and substance and the dress clings to her figure with a deliciously precarious grip. She sits across the table from me on what I suppose is our first date. There is a candle between us; its light glints on the restaurant cutlery.

Anna's screams still reverberate through my head. It started when I told her that Janet was going to look after her again because I had to go out. The sound was a howl of despair, of utter desolation. She clung to me, she pummelled me with her tiny fists and would not calm even when, in sheer desperation, I gripped her tightly and shouted at her. Janet, thank God, took charge and urged me to be gone.

"Are you okay?" Miriam sounds worried. Christ, she thinks I'm having second thoughts about her.

"Anna was a bit upset."

"It's only natural." There's that word again.

"I suppose so."

"She has no mother, so she's clinging to you, Rob. She'll be all right. It'll just take time."

A pause.

"So what do you do for a living?" Miriam asks.

"You mean I haven't told you yet?"

"That must make you unique as a man. One complete party and forty minutes of a date and you still haven't told me about your career and how important it is and how important *you* are."

"That's because it's not very exciting. I'm a lab technician. I do nasty things to rats and mice." I notice her expression and add hastily; "Medical research."

"Do you think it's necessary?" She sounds more curious than angry. "Animal experimentation, I mean."

"Yes, I think it is. We have to test new drugs on living organisms at some point."

"You seem too..." She shrugs. "What I mean is I would have thought you were a doctor or something. It's...I don't know, your demeanour. The way you talk."

"It's about all I can cope with at the moment."

"What, torturing little animals?"

"How else will we know?"

"But surely animal physiology is different to human."

I panic slightly, not liking the way this has reared up between us. It could be a point of friction, if not open dispute, in the future.

Future?

Miriam reaches across to lay her hand on mine. "It's okay. I'm playing devil's advocate."

She keeps her hand there. It's hot and the contact fires tiny electric shocks into my groin.

"It really is just a job. Since…Since Chrissie died I've needed something less intense. I'm at home in the lab environment so this job is perfect."

Miriam shrugs. "I understand, I suppose. I've never lost someone close so what do I know?"

"As much as I did until it happened."

"Anna will be okay," Miriam says again. "You're entitled to a life of your own."

"It was cancer," I hear myself say and wonder why I'm telling her this.

Miriam starts but her hand remains in place.

"In her liver," I add. "The GP thought it was a gall-stone. By the time they found out what it really was, it was too late." The dénouement of my story is weak, anti-climactic. I feel a squeeze from Miriam's hand and I realise that I'm a fraud, enjoying sympathy where none is deserved.

You'd think it would be easy. Especially as Miriam is enthusiastic and skilled and squeezed into the kind of black basque and stockings you only normally see in the pages of a soft porn glossy.

But here I am, in her bed, naked and desolate, eyes fixed on the ceiling. Miriam kneels beside me. "It doesn't matter," she says in a tone that means that it does. It's been a long time for her as well. And this isn't our first attempt.

"I can't fucking relax."

"You can't relax to fuck."

We both chuckle. Our laughter is brief.

"You should go home. You're worried about Anna."

Yes I am. She screamed again tonight. She screams every time I go out of the house.

"Perhaps we should take things more slowly."

Panicked, I turn to look at her. "What do you mean?"

"I think you're too hurt to...well, to rush into this." She touches my face. "Don't look so worried. I'm not suggesting we break-up. I really want this. We just have to be patient. The right moment will come." She chuckles again. "Then so will you."

The joke is awful but it works.

"Rob," She's serious again. "What if Anna were to meet me?"

"No, no it's too soon..."

"I'm sure she's not stupid. She may only be six but I bet she suspects something. You must reek of my perfume when you get home."

"She's not my wife." *Christ, oh Christ why did I say that?*

"No, but she must recognise perfume as a sign that there's another woman in your life, a rival, a threat."

Too much, I want to get out of this bed, away from this conversation. My heart thud-thuds, my breathing shallows.

"One moment you're always there, the next you're going out twice, three times a week. She's already lost one parent."

Please shut up. Please.

"I think we should all meet up. Stop the subterfuge."

I don't know.

"Let's make it somewhere neutral. We could act as if we're just friends, keep it light. If Anna gets too upset, I'll make my excuses and go."

There is logic in the idea. Seeing Miriam as a normal human being could possibly remove the sting. Besides, Anna might actually like her.

I hesitate a moment longer. Then give in.

"Okay, okay we'll try it, Saturday afternoon, in the park. Anna likes feeding the ducks. There's a tearoom near the lake. I could 'just happen to meet you' there. Good plan?"

"Good plan." A pause.

I clamber out of the bed. "I'll see you on Thursday then..."

"No, not this Thursday."

"But why?"

"I need a break. I'm sorry, it's all a bit...you know."

"Yeah," I feign understanding. "Yeah, of course."

The taste of her gentle rejection is bitter. We're at a crisis point and I don't want to be at any crisis points. I've had my share of crisis points. I want a simple, unfettered relationship with this woman who makes me feel so good.

There's nothing for it but to go home, which I do, feeling bleak, tired. I tell myself it's an overreaction. I'll see Miriam on Saturday, but the teenage, lonely-man part of me won't settle for that.

The trap is set, all the actors are in place, two of the three players primed for their chance encounter at the quaint, wooden tearoom in the park. I chain-smoke and carry a plastic bag filled with out-of-date bread, dry but not yet mouldy. Anna's hand is in mine. My heart pumps loudly, my mouth is dry. A few hardy souls, bundled in coats, faces pinched, are seated at the outside tables. I can't see Miriam.

She's stood me up. She's had second thoughts...

There, at one of the more remote tables, disguised in a thick quilted coat with its fur-edged hood pulled over her head. She is looking away from us, staring out across the boating lake.

"I want to feed the ducks," Anna lets go of my hand.

Something must have snagged Miriam's attention because she turns.

She waves. I see her smile, broad and contrived. I want to hold her tight, I want to kiss her. I don't want to care about Anna.

I don't want my face shoved into my mistake any longer.

"Who's that?" Anna asks, alarmed.

"I think it's...yes...its Miriam." I was never much of an actor.

"The lady you've been going to see?"

She's too bloody sharp. Her perceptiveness unnerves me.

"Is she your girlfriend?" Anna makes the word sound like a bad taste.

"Don't be silly. Come on, let's say hello."

She shakes her head.

"She won't bite you?"

Anna draws in close.

"Just hello."

"No."

Suddenly impatient, I give her a tug. I am desperate for this to work because I want to move on with Miriam and not be held back by this child.

"Hi," says Miriam. "Out for a walk?" She's a better actor than me.

"We're going to feed the ducks." I hold up the bag of bread; the gesture feels lame.

"And who is this?" Addressed to Anna. All so bright, all so friendly-loud and dripping mock surprise.

"Anna."

"Hello, Anna."

"Say hi to Miriam." I urge.

"No," says Anna and she means it, Christ how she means it.

She hauls back on my hand.

"Don't worry," says Miriam and I can see that she is hurt. I hate that hurt. "Some other time."

"Come on, Anna," I urge, teeth gritted behind my own fake smile. "Stop being so rude."

"I hate her. I hate you!" This last to Miriam who flinches. "You're a bitch!"

"Anna!"

"I hate her." Voice rising, becoming shrill. "She wants to take you away from me."

Miriam's face pales, though her smile remains intact.

She shrugs, the gesture minute but intimate. Anna sees it and somehow understands what it means, sees the link it represents. And suddenly she is screaming and pummelling my arm with her free hand. I feel like crying myself because *I* did this, because I thought it was the best way, but now I know what a fucking mistake it all was and there is nothing I can do because people are looking.

Miriam is distressed but handling it the best she can. She gets to her feet, picks up her handbag from the wooden table.

No. no Miriam, it's okay. Please.

Her eyes are red-rimmed. "I think it best… you know, best if I go…"

And I know what *go* means.

I watch her hurry away. She doesn't look round. I simply stand, staring after her, unable to offer any comfort to Anna as she sobs. People look at me, accusingly, judging me.

You don't know the half of it, I yell at them silently. You know fuck all.

For a moment I wonder if Miriam is in, despite the light burning in the hallway and visible through the frosted glass of her front door. I'm relieved. I'm crushed with frustration. I don't know what to expect. My breathing is shallow, my heart pounds. I shiver, and not entirely because of the cold burrowing though my clothes.

A silhouette appears at the door. Its arm rises, the lock rattles.

"Rob?" She doesn't sound pleased to see me, but neither does she sound hostile.

Miriam's hair is dishevelled, her eyes look red. She wears a black roll neck sweater that seems to drown her and emphasise the paleness of her face. Her feet are bare. I smell alcohol.

She doesn't invite me in.

My mouth opens to produce a pathetic "Look, I'm sorry about this afternoon…"

"I can't cope with this right now…"

"I have to talk to you."

"It's too complicated."

She makes to shut the door. I think she's crying.

I force my way into the doorway.

Miriam shakes her head, and, yes, she *is* crying. "Don't Rob, please go home."

"I… I love you Miriam…"

She freezes, stares at me and I can't decide if she is appalled or euphoric. My strength seems to drain and I no longer have the energy to even lift my head to look at her.

Then she falls into my arms and a sort of madness is on us and we collapse onto the floor of her hallway and I kick the door shut behind me and rip at her jeans and she rips at mine and she offers herself to me and, at last, I enter her and she crushes me so hard to herself I'm afraid I'll smother her.

When I finally roll away, the floor is hard under my back and the hall light is bright in my eyes. Miriam lays her head on my chest and we rest in silence.

After a while she says; "Do you want a drink?

"No, thanks. I have to go."

She looks up at me and chuckles. "Why? Are you going to turn into a pumpkin if you don't get home by midnight?"

"I have to get back..." I hesitate, then grit my teeth and say it. "To Anna."

"Oh for God's sake, no wonder she's such a princess, you can't be at her beck and call the whole time. Besides, that babysitter of yours will be all right for a little longer."

"Janet isn't there."

I feel Miriam stiffen.

"What do you mean *isn't there*? Who is looking after Anna, Rob?"

"Janet can't cope with her anymore."

"Who is looking after Anna?" Miriam is on her knees. "Jesus! You left her? *Alone*? Your own daughter?"

"I had to see you. I couldn't leave things broken..."

Miriam pulls away from me. "Oh God just go. Please, go away. Now."

There's nothing I can say. I stand and pull on my jeans. Miriam doesn't look at me but stays on her knees, arms wrapped about herself, staring at the wall. The panic hits when I lurch from the house into the icy rain.

Anna is still asleep when I get home. Relief brings reaction. I slump into an armchair, grinding the heels of my hands into my forehead. *Christ, Christ, Christ.*

I must have fallen asleep, because suddenly the telephone rings and the sound is shocking. Disorientated, I snatch up the receiver. My voice is bleary and hoarse. "Yes?"

"It's me." Miriam's voice is hard.

"Thank God—"

"You left your wallet here. It must have fallen out of your pocket"

"Ah, thanks."

"I saw your driving licence."

Shit.

"The photograph is you but the name is Dr Stephen Thomas."

I can explain I say silently, but lack the strength to actually speak the words.

"I recognised the name, the way I thought I recognised you when we first met at Alan and Kat's. So I looked it up, a quick Google. Do you know what I found?"

Yes, I do.

"Doctor Stephen Thomas of the Hartford Institute for Genetic Studies. Dr Thomas who resigned amid rumours of unlicensed experimentation. They said it was pressure, because your wife was terminally ill. But there were rumours, hotly denied I might add, that you and your team had *completed* something and that's the real reason you left. You're mentioned on a handful of conspiracy theory sites. They make some outrageous claims." A pause. "You sick bastard. You *did* create—"

"No, no Miriam, I'm not God, it wasn't like that..."

But the line is dead.

Wasn't it?

I want Miriam.

A mad professor who played the God who giveth and taketh away...

The roar of blood fills my head. I am dead, yet someone is screaming in there, from deep inside the white rage, clawing for release I cannot grant because if I do everything will break.

Christ, Christ, Christ...

I wake Anna early.

"We're going out," I say. "We'll just have breakfast then we'll go for a drive and a walk, to our special place."

I leave her to dress. Outside the windows, grey sky bleeds cold drizzle. Downstairs, I prepare cereal then fetch our coats. I select the bright blue one for Anna. It's her best coat, reserved for special occasions.

THINK BELSEN

"Think Belsen," said the glossies. "Extreme-crop is the must-have of the season; show off those prominent bones and that concave midriff. Forget tits and bums; ribs and scapula are the new cleavage."

"Fink Belsen," proclaimed professional celebrity Verity Blane, self-starved into a wheelchair and example to women everywhere. "Less is more right? So who was less than all? You know, them in Belsen. It's sort of the ultimate. What every woman attains for."

Thinking Belsen, however, didn't prevent Anna Meade from setting off a low-grade alarm as she followed her best friend into the Normal Woman Mall. She froze, sunken cheeks aflame as the warning voice oozed prettily from the door speaker.

"I'm sorry, but you may not match the size criteria set by the retail outlets in this building."

"It was probably your sweater," said Cherry, leaning on her Gucci walking stick, shaven-headed and gorgeously gaunt. She shivered in the extreme-crop she wore. Her ribs rose and fell like the folds of an accordion as she panted for breath. Cherry was always ready with an encouraging word, no matter how stupid you had been, and surely coming back to the mall a mere six weeks after childbirth qualified as stupid.

Cherry had a point about the sweater. Its mohair filaments were fluffed-up enough to have brushed the sensor.

"Maybe," Cherry looked suddenly awkward, "you know, maybe we should split up and meet for coffee in Aztec in an hour."

Anna didn't want to split up. This was her first mall-time for almost three months. She needed Cherry at her side.

"I mean," Cherry went on. "I've got, like, some so-boring shopping to do before we get down to the real work." She was lying wasn't she? The alarm had rattled her. "See you in an hour Anna, in Aztec, yeah?"

And she was gone, melded into the amorphous hurry of paste-fleshed, grave-thin shoppers.

Panicked, Anna wondered if she should make her escape now and go to the Outsize (Fat Pig) Mall instead. No shame in it. Some women couldn't maintain size-minus, especially after childbirth. God, some women never achieved it at all. At least she had been a size-minus once, the result of focus, sacrifice and three emergency hospitalisations.

No.

She – correction, her sweater – had barely brushed the sides of the door. The main alarm had not sounded. Anna Meade had every right to be here.

Reassuringly hunger-dizzy, she set off towards the main concourse. Leaning heavily on her Miss Selfridge, pearl-headed cane, she shuffled bravely past the Great Escalator as it sighed frail, featherlight human burdens through the mall's five levels of retail Nirvana. Music soothed and excited, lyrics interlaced with subliminal suggestion. Giant screens played the latest music vids and the latest ads – in most cases, one and the same.

And repeated, over and over was the critically-acclaimed Think Belson ad for No-Food Yoghurt.

EXTERIOR

Age-greyed, real-life footage of a concentration camp. Shaven-headed, cadaverous figures gaze, dead-eyed from behind barbed wire.

Cut to–

INTERIOR

Actor-models KARA KING and NATISHA WEN stand at a large

table, sorting through a pile of clothes, shoes and suitcases. The two actors wear the standard striped prison tunics, unbuttoned enough to show off cleavage and prominent ribs. They are superimposed onto a real-life background. The table is stock footage although the section nearest to the actors is a prop, blended into the real article. The colour scheme is the same ancient monochrome quality as the stock footage. Other prisoners are glimpsed at the same table.

KARA
Straightens and wipes her brow.
Strands of hair stick fetchingly to her face.
God I'm so hungry.
(*Sound; slight crackly quality to suggest genuine soundtrack*)

Cut to Natisha, who does not look up from her work when she speaks.

NATISHA
Don't be such a weakling. If they can do it,
(*Cut back to stock footage: A group of emaciated prisoners sorting through*
the same pile of belongings)
so can we.

KARA
But I can't fight it this time.

NATISHA
(*Smiling with benign tolerance*)
All right.
(*Reaches inside her tunic to produce a small plastic pot*)
I've got one last No-Food.

KARA
(*Alarmed*)
But it's yoghurt!

NATISHA

No-Food's a treat you can eat without ingesting any foodstuff whatsoever.

KARA

(*Taking and opening the pot*)
But what about you?

NATISHA

Willpower and vision. But sometimes I am a little tempted.
(*Giggling, she dips her finger in the now open pot and licks it guiltily*)

Kara knocks her hand away playfully then turns to see her fellow prisoners and her grin turns to guilt. Tearfully, and with stoic generosity, she holds out the pot towards the camera. A hand appears in shot to receive it. A glimpse of striped prison tunic sleeve is seen.

VOICEOVER

No-Food. We all need a little help sometimes.

Kara King claimed that those tears were real and that the one minute ad was the hardest acting role she had ever undertaken. Anna believed her.

Anna decided to start her shopping in *Sin*, a cornucopia of size-minus couture, and ruthlessly strict about the dimensions of its clientele. A foolish choice for a comeback, but walking into Aztec with a carrier bag bearing the famous logo (halo over the "S", the "n" formed into the three prongs of a Devil's pitchfork) would prove to Cherry that mohair really had triggered the warning in the Normal Woman's entrance.

Anna stopped to let an electro-chair glide past. Its owner nodded her thanks, the gesture obviously painful, the effort etched into a face made masculine by the absence of feature-forming fat.

Vile fat, foul fat, disgusting, filthy fat.

Yellow it was. Anna had seen it on *Fat-Killers*. The presenter had scooped a ladle-full out of a bowl. "How could we ever let such filth grow in our bodies?"

Fat, she said, was a disease.

Anna hesitated at *Sin's* entrance. If she brushed the sides of this door, an alarm would definitely sound out her shame.

You are not fat, she told herself. You have given birth to a child and now, six weeks later, you are in the mall wearing the same clothes you bought in this very shop before you fell pregnant. A little tight perhaps, but the same clothes.

So come on.

She twisted sideways, the action instinctive, and risky, because it was cheating and, as such, bound to be picked up by the door's profile sensors. She closed her eyes, stepped through.

And felt nothing, not the slightest contact.

Safe, dignity intact, she waited for her breathing to steady into its usual laboured gasp. She gazed about the shop. *Sin* was always a wonder, a place of hush, decorated with lush drapery, mosaic and sculpture. Classical music whispered from hidden speakers while customers worked the clothes racks in reverent silence, the only sound they made the occasional hum of an electro-chair and rattle of hangers.

Anna took a step towards the nearest display.

"Madam." An assistant cut into her path. The woman leaned on her walking stick, hand trembling, face drawn deliciously tight over her skull, skin jaundiced to an attractive yellow. "I'm very sorry." She spoke in a near-whisper, the soul of tact. "The alarm."

"But...it didn't..."

"Our alarms are discreet. We don't like scenes here at *Sin*. I am sorry."

Sorry, translated as *serves you right you weak-willed cow*.

Other shoppers looked up and round. Stares bore in, someone sniggered.

"My sweater..." Anna plucked a handful of mohair from the sleeve.

"Madam, I don't think you'll find what you are looking for here."

A smile appeared, painted in glistening lipstick, a smile that barely hid fang and viper-tongue.

"I...I'm sorry...I uh..."

Anna stumbled, backwards, the rejection so physical it was like being pushed. She rushed out through the door. Dizzy, crying, she barged a tall, cadaverous mother who tugged her corpse-pale daughter close and hurried away. Crowds swirled, the vid screens blared.

NATISHA
Don't be such a weakling. If they can do it,
(*Cut back to stock footage: A group of emaciated prisoners sorting through the same pile of belongings*)
so can we...

Anna glimpsed the *Aztec Coffee Café*.

Which was all but full. One table left, by the toilet door. Anna hurried through the clutches of the skin-on-bone elite who had gathered to converse in a furious, strenuously cultivated display of easy friendship. She collapsed into the remaining seat and waited to be served.

No sign of Cherry, thank god, because Anna had not one bag to show for her time here.

The waitress arrived, patiently impatient.

"Skinny latte, no milk, no caffeine, no sweetener, not too much flavour and only a hint of colour. Oh, and a Full Comfort Platter, thanks."

It was all right to indulge in here. Every table had a vomit bowl, and a long wooden throat probe was part of the cutlery.

Laughter, chatter, the long groan of vomiting and splash of regurgitated food, followed, of course, by the hiss of odour-sweet spray and gurgle of the auto-flush.

They knew. All of them.

That one, dabbing puke from the corners of her scarlet-rimmed mouth, her in the wheelchair who could hardly turn her head to look, the teenage princess over by the wall, peevish in her stomach-cramped, starvation agonies. They could smell Anna's failure, could smell the fat flowing through her, robbing her of shape and form.

Anna sipped her newly arrived beverage, closed her eyes against the coffee-tainted water taste. She made to replace the cup on its saucer, but missed the table altogether and suddenly her skin-jeans were scalding hot and wet.

"Fuck!" she cried out and surged to her feet.

She ran, crashing out of *Aztec*, back out into the sea of bobbing, twisting heads with their long hair, short hair and chemo-baldness—

That stopped her.

Think Belsen...

No longer enough.

If they can do it so can we...

Real commitment was needed, a Verity Blane-style sacrifice.

Expensive, but some things were more important than money.

Will renewed, Anna left the Mall by the thoughtfully discreet emergency exit (the Shame Door) which she had never, ever used before.

~

Anna felt better once she was inside Ultra-Med. It was, after all, a chemist and pharmacy, which meant that all sizes were welcome to pass through its non-alarmed doors; from the limping, breathless size-minus and uncomfortably curved size tens and twelves to the positively obese fourteens and sixteens.

Anna found an assistant, a middle-aged, gaunt-faced beauty, who smiled a mouth-wide smile.

"How can I help, love?" she asked, eyes hard and searching. They added a silent *you fat pig* to the question.

"I..." How could she admit to such failure as this? "I had a baby and now I can't seem to lose any more weight."

"Have you tried Felladine? Thin-Eze?"

Each time a nod, a mumbled yes.

"I understand there's something else..."

How many women asked that same question after the mandatory have-you-tried list?

"You mean the cancer pill."

Jesus, the word was like a club, a knife.

"Does it work?"

"The success rate is eight-five percent."

"Do you really lose weight when you have...when the pills are working?"

"Oh yes, absolutely, but you need to be sure, love. It's a big commitment"

"I'm sure." Was she? "Do...do I need medical help or anything? A prescription?"

"No. All you have to decide is breast or bowel."

"I'm sorry?"

"What sort of cancer do you want?"

"I...I hadn't thought of that."

"Not many do."

"What do you think?"

"I'm not allowed to think, but..." A quick glance about the shop then a conspiratorial lean forward and wave for Anna to come closer. "Bowel is better. Breast could result in you losing...you know."

"Oh, yes, of course."

"There are risks."

Terrible, inconceivable risks in fact. But there were risks to being fat. Heart failure, they said, and social ostracism.

Anna nodded. "Bowel then," she said.

The assistant reached behind the counter and produced an innocuous carton with an all-but unpronounceable name printed on the front.

"How much?" Anna asked, mouth dried by the reality of the little cardboard box.

The answer drove the air from her lungs.

"You'll need a course of chemo-tabs as well."

"No... I can't afford..."

"You'll die without them."

The assistant produced the second box.

If they can do it so can we...

"I... I need to talk to my husband first." Anna said.

"Take your time, love, it's a big decision."

Anna fumbled for her phone then quick-dialled home.

She could hear the wall-vid in the lounge where Jason was, no doubt, sprawled on the sofa where he spent every Saturday afternoon. A football crowd chanted. Jason belched.

"Hi Jase, its Anna."

"Yeah?"

His eyes would be locked onto the screen, one puffy hand curled about the phone, the other about a beer can. Empties would be scattered around him, eviscerated snack bags spread over the carpet, spewing their crumbs onto the pile.

"How's Shanna?"

"Asleep – oh fuck fuck. Bloody hell, how could he have missed that?"

The crowd roared in sympathetic frustration – and joy in the case of the opposition.

Of course Shanna would still be asleep, the Mum-Free drops in her noon time feed were guaranteed to provide four hours of mall-time for Mum and footie time for Dad.

"Jase, I need some extra cash."

"Yeah."

"Shanna... I'm going to have to... I mean, it's best if we do it now, before we get too attached to her, and we can always have another child."

"Yeah."

"One of the drug research institutes would be best. They're always advertising for volunteers and unwanted... you know... They pay well too. Not that Shanna's unwanted, not by me anyway. She's not is she? Jase? Is she?"

"Nah – Wanker!"

Crowd roar, several thousand agreeing with Jason's assessment of the player in question.

"She'll be looked after. Better than she is now probably. We're both... you know... just so busy aren't we?"

"Yeah."

"I only have to sign an e-form in the shop. They'll probably be round to collect her before I get home."

"Right."

"You will be there, won't you?"

"Yeah, yeah...ah shit. What the fuck is wrong with those bastards?"

Milk, Shanna smelled of milk and some sweetness Anna could never describe.

"Kiss her for me; tell her I love her, won't you?"

"Yeah."

"I'll...I'll see you later."

"Yeah, right."

She hung up.

Turned back to the counter. The assistant had already produced a form-pad.

"Just put your forefinger on the screen, love."

Warm, Shanna was always warm, her skin, so soft it didn't feel like real skin but something made to be kissed and touched and held.

Anna stared at the pad and the mind-roar began. *Oh Jesus, Jesus, Christ, Oh God...* She looked at the assistant, whose smile remained firmly in place, then at the pad and made the only decision possible.

A Child is a Woman's

"Maria Carr?" I said, knocking on the door to her room at the women's refuge. "My name is Heather Moore. I'm a social worker. I've been asked to come to see you."

"Please...Please leave us alone."

"I'm afraid I can't. There are concerns for your child."

"Bethany's fine." Right on cue, an infant began to cry.

"I'm sure she is." I shouted above Bethany's wailing. "But I must speak with you, if only to prove that everything *is* okay."

A pause, then the door opened to reveal a slight-built woman with a pleasant face made haggard by fear. A neglected mane of auburn hair tumbled over her shoulders. Her eyes were dark-ringed, and she seemed frail, as if diminished by whatever troubles had driven her to this place.

"You might as well come in," she muttered. "Seeing as I have no choice."

I perched myself on the edge of the bed and waited patiently as Maria shushed her daughter to sleep, then laid her on the duvet beside me. The child settled. Maria wandered to the window and peeked through a chink in the drawn curtains.

"So, do you think you can help?" she said, turning to face me.

"If you'll let me."

A laugh, short and bitter. "Oh I'd let you. You can have it all. But I can't. I..." It was Maria's turn to cry, arms folded about herself, bent double as if in pain.

"I know you're running away," I offered gently. "You wouldn't be here otherwise."

"If you mean from a violent husband, I dealt with *that* one a long time ago."

I paused. "Why not tell me about it?"

"You'd have me Sectioned."

"Try me."

There was another pause, this one tight with indecision. Bethany murmured in her sleep. Maria sighed, more tears threatened.

"It was a house," she said.

Which seemed appropriate, because Maria Carr was an estate agent, just divorced and recently returned to her old career. Unfortunately, in the two months she had been at Carter and Knight's, she had made no sales whatsoever. The impossibly youthful branch manager had *spoken* with her about it, his threats veiled behind a fog of management gibberish.

On that November afternoon, the afternoon it began, rain beat on the Agency's plate glass window, melting the street scene beyond into molten, monochrome drab. Time crawled. Maria's phone remained obstinately silent.

"Good afternoon,"

Startled, she looked up to see two expensive-looking coats, modelled by what she could only describe as an expensive-looking, middle-aged couple; one partner was stunningly blonde, the other square-jawed. Both of them were perfectly tanned.

"We're rather interested in one of the properties advertised in your window," the man said.

Maria's heart lifted.

"Number Ten, Dalton Street," the woman added.

Maria's heart sank. "Number...Yes, yes of course. I'll just get the details."

Forcing a smile and business-like briskness, she crossed to the filing cabinet. Oh hell! She cursed silently. Why Dalton Street? So far no one had so much as made an offer for the place; a couple of prospects hadn't even bothered to go through the front door.

The customers, who had by now introduced themselves as Robert and Caroline Weatherly, gave the leaflet only a cursory glance. "We'd like to take a look," Robert said. "As soon as possible, now if it's convenient."

Maria reached for her diary and affected a *now*-might-not-be-easy-frown as she studied the blank page.

~

Dalton Street was place of faded glories; a long, gently sloping road bordered by towering three-storey town houses on one side and detached Victorian properties on the other. Most of the town houses were now bedsits, their paint peeling and loud music leaking through closed sash widows. The detached houses, however, had fared better. Except for Number Ten.

Maria winced as she swung her car into the drive. The Weatherlys could *not* be serious. In the prematurely fading light, the property looked morose and desolate. The windows were boarded against vandals, the garden overgrown, the pseudo-classical statuettes lining the drive lichen-encrusted and weather-worn.

The Weatherly's Mercedes crunched to halt beside Maria's ancient Fiesta. Caroline got out first and stared at the house as if transfixed. When Maria had manoeuvred herself, her paperwork and the key out of her own car, she saw that Caroline was smiling. Her eyes shone.

Maria unlocked the heavy, weather-warped front door then fumbled the brass light switch. The hall was suddenly draped in wan yellow. Mouldering carpets and tattered wallpaper were revealed. Sighing, she prepared herself for that falsely non-committal "Mmmm." They all did it, all those DIY-enthusiasts and bargain-hungry builders. "Mmmm" – roughly translated as "What a pile of shite."

But Caroline was already striding towards the stairs.

"They're sound," Maria reassured them as she hurried in pursuit. "And this hall, very spacious."

"Mmmmm" Caroline said, but it was a different "Mmmm".

She bounded up the steps, blonde hair a-shimmer even in this light, exclaiming that it was all simply *gorgeous*. Robert trotted in her wake. There was a turn in the stair, the post decorated by an age-greened bronze statuette of a cherub clutching a glass globe from which an electric lamp glowed feebly.

Robert rounded the corner and froze, leaving Caroline to finish her ascent alone and Maria to almost collide with his broad back. He twisted round, frowning. "Can you hear it?" he asked quietly.

"Hear what?" Maria asked.

Robert shook his head, shrugged. "Nothing, it doesn't matter. What's that first room up there?"

"The bathroom."

"Okay, thanks," and he was on his way.

Maria made to follow.

And there was the sound, growing out of the musty silence, bringing with it a shock of freezing air on clothes-protected flesh.

Creak... Creak... it went. Creak... Creak.

"May we go in?" Robert called down to her. The Weatherlys were hesitating at the bathroom door.

"Sorry? Oh, yes go ahead. Feel free, take a good look around." Maria hoped her voice was not too tremulous. Something must have showed through, however, because Robert studied her carefully before he disappeared into the bathroom.

Maria paused on the stairs to give herself time to recover. She was shaking, though she didn't know why. She had been in this house several times, both with clients and alone. Big, old, empty buildings did not frighten her. They were simply boxes formed from walls, floors and ceilings. The noises they made were the groans and complaints of age. The shadows they contained, just shadows.

Creak... Creak...

The sound broke her inertia and she hurried into the bathroom.

Caroline was studying the room carefully, touching dank walls, running her gloved fingertips over the rim of the ancient and stained bath, staring into each shadowed corner. Robert hung back, hands in pockets, somehow hunched into himself. Maria caught his eye again and saw...fear?

The tour continued. Maria opened endless doors to display endless mouldering rooms, each tainted by the perfume of long-trapped, moisture-laden air. And while his wife examined and enthused, Robert stayed near each threshold, increasingly ill-at-ease.

Maria's own heart steam-hammered, her head throbbed, inexplicable tears welled. She wanted to glance over her shoulder, she wanted to cry. But most of all, she wanted to get out.

Creak... Creak... Louder now, the sound echoed through the hollow rooms, danced shadows about the periphery of Maria's vision, drove fists of breath-stealing anxiety into her stomach.

Creak... Creak...

She had to stop this. She was with clients. The clients were interested. This was real life; the rest was mind-tricks, exhaustion. Then nausea welled, she reeled dizzily, shivered. All signs of imminent...

Outside it was completely dark, the garden a formless, sodden tangle that clawed and clutched and lashed as Maria followed the alarmed Caroline Weatherly out of the front door to where Robert was vomiting into the bushes.

Shaken, Maria turned towards the house. The door was open, spilling light into a dark that seemed to swallow it whole. She knew then that she could never go back in there.

Trying to pull herself together, she asked Robert if he was alright.

"Yes," he answered groggily. "Yes, I'm fine...so stupid."

"Perhaps you should come inside." Caroline sounded worried. "Sit on the stairs for a moment."

"No!" Robert snapped so fiercely that both Caroline and Maria flinched back from him. "I'm sorry." He softened. "I'm just... just tired, that's all. I'll wait out here in the fresh air while you finish looking round."

"Actually, I don't need to see any more," Caroline said.

I'll bet you don't, Maria answered, silent and resigned.

"I've made up my mind," Caroline added firmly. "I want this house."

~

Maria lived in a flat on the third floor of a squat brick cube, located on the edge of the town centre. The echoing, concrete stairs were a steep climb, but Maria comforted herself with the thought that this daily ascent saved her the expense of attending a gym. Tonight, however, she barely noticed the upward trek, despite her tiredness and despite the weight of Bethany, retrieved from the child minder and nestled against her hip. Tonight, she was happy, high, positively delirious.

She had achieved what none of her colleagues had been able to achieve; all-but sold That House.

As always, Bethany was in her bouncer and the kettle boiling before Maria had even taken off her coat. Routine was important. Routine kept her sane. Babies were demanding, the flat was cold and cramped, the view poor. And she was lonely. God, how lonely. But, at last, things seemed to be on an upward turn.

A sale meant commission, and the possibility of keeping her job. That alone would get her out of this wretched flat and into a house. God, she wanted that for Bethany more than anything else.

"A child..."

The voice was a fingertip trail over her neck. She spun round. The kitchenette was empty.

Shaken, she busied herself with Bethany's bottle. There were no voices, okay? She was under pressure, exhausted. Maria gathered up baby milk and coffee mug and made for the door. She switched off the light.

"A child is..."

The words spun her round again to see—

A figure at the window – the *third floor* window – vivid against the dark; female, wild-haired, wild-eyed – then Maria's own image, door-framed and silhouetted by the light from the hallway beyond.

Bethany cried, her shrieks shocking in the silence. Startled, Maria shouted "Stop it!" Then, ashamed, held the child to herself. She had heard and seen *nothing*.

Nothing.

Then another sound drilled into the maelstrom of Bethany's crying, insistent, relentless.

Creak... Creak...

~

The following day, Robert Weatherly phoned Carter and Knight's. Steeling herself against disappointment, Maria picked up her receiver to take the transferred call.

"Hello? Maria? Look, this is going to sound a bit strange, but it's about the house."

No, it won't sound strange. You've changed your mind. Everyone else does, so why should you be any different?

"My wife is besotted with the place, has all kinds of plans for it. I don't want to let her down, but..." Hesitation, a struggle for the right words. "Quite frankly, the place gave me the willies. That attack of sickness... I'm sorry, I must sound half crazy."

"Not at all." *Was it a creaking sound, Mr Weatherly? Is that what frightened you?*

"It's all in my mind of course." A nervous chuckle. "Look, I've got to get over this...this phobia, so I'd like another look round. We're up from London again on Friday, so could you oblige?"

Of course she could oblige. Friday it was, two pm.

Only *she* didn't want to go back there either. When Maria replaced the receiver, her breathing was shallow, her heart pounded. She *couldn't* go back. She could *not*...

So, she was going to let her own stupidity lose this sale, was she? She grabbed the diary and made the entry. *We'll cure this together, Mr Robert Weatherly. Therapy starts on Friday at 2pm.*

~

The evening was bad.

Maria was jumpy as she climbed the stairway to her flat, startled by shadows, by her own echoes, waiting for the temperature to drop, for voices, for that *sound*. She almost fled to her parents. But that would mean that she had lost. This stupid tension was nothing more sinister than single-parent strain, hormones perhaps. Post-natal depression even.

Noise was best; the radio in the kitchen, the television in the tiny box that called itself a lounge, because, whenever there was silence, the creaking began, distant, peripheral, never there when listened for, creeping back when ignored.

Maria slept with the radio on. Voices and music infiltrated her dreams, their rhythm set by a metronome that didn't tick but creaked—

She woke, suddenly, shivering despite the duvet, despite the central heating. Small hours easy-listening drifted from her bedside radio as she lay, disorientated, unsure why she was afraid. Then Bethany screamed, a piercing shriek of a terror that no infant should ever unleash. Driven by raw instinct, Maria was up and lurching into the passage, towards the open door of Bethany's room.

"A child is a woman's, no matter the father," Bethany yelled in an obscene rasping of underdeveloped vocal chords.

Maria stumbled to a halt. She had heard, oh God she had heard…

Crying with fear, loathing and rage, Maria burst into the bedroom. Light on, she rushed to the cot, where the child lay on her back, covers kicked into a crumpled heap by her tiny feet. She was still crying, minute fists clenched, her breath puffs of condensation in the chill.

Maria leaned over the cot rail to pick her up.

And the creaking started, in this room, here.

Creak… Creak…

Maria snatched up her daughter. The sound grew. In here, *here*, above her head. The room was suddenly full of rhythmically arcing shadow. To and fro it swung, to and fro, in time to that familiar hell-beat, its slipstream a disturbance of frozen air that danced against her flesh.

And dragged lightly through her hair.

She screamed and stumbled back.

Creak… Creak…

Bethany squirmed in her grasp. Maria looked down to see the baby face staring back up at her, eyes old and grave. "A child is a woman's, no matter the father," she croaked. "A child is a woman's, no matter the father. A child is a woman's, no matter the father…"

Maria wrenched the baby away from herself, shrieking at her to stop it, stop it, STOP IT!

~

Hollowed out by shock, aching from a night spent, foetus curled and afraid, on the floor of Bethany's bedroom, Maria sat in a side office at Preston Gillespie, Solicitors, and pulled at the ribbon holding together a bloated collection of documents. Reading through the deeds to Number Ten Dalton Street was, she knew, the final admission of madness. But she had to find…what? Some concrete evidence that the visitations were hallucinations?

Or that they were real?

The house was built in 1887, on land purchased by its first owner, James Bury. He died in 1898, and his widow had sold the property in the April of that year to a Mrs Susannah Gemling, herself the widow of Colonel George Gemling. Susannah died in September 1898, intestate.

An old lady then, intending to live out her final years in Dalton Street, only it turned out to be her last months.

More names, an endless list (because no one had stayed in that house for long) following the years and decades through an entire century. But always Maria's eyes slid back to Susannah Gemling; just a name, letters in faded ink that represented a human being who was gone forever.

Months, that was the connection. Something Maria had been living with for the best part of the previous year; nine months, eight months...

Maria re-tied the ancient paperwork and set off for the Agency. She was supposed to be at work, not chasing ghosts.

There it was. The word she had been avoiding all this time.

Distracted, she drove badly through the rain-blurred town. There was a roundabout, the Agency was off the second exit, but the first would take her to the library. She didn't want to go there, did she? She needed to get back to work, now, before she was missed...

Maria found what she was looking for quickly, thank God, because she had only allowed herself one hour here in the library.

It was a lurid headline in a September 1898 edition of one of the county's more breathless dailies: "Terrible Death of Young Widow."

Young widow...

"On the afternoon of the 21st September, a Mr Herbert Miller, occasional gardener at Number 10 Dalton Street, became much exercised when he was unable to find his employer, Mrs Susannah Gemling, to whom he wished to report some minor matter pertaining to his duties. Mrs Gemling was, it appears, something of a recluse and seldom left the house. Accordingly, her absence from the premises was of grave concern to her gardener.

"A thorough search of the premises was concluded in the cellar, where

Mr Miller discovered his employer hanging, lifeless, by her neck—"

Creak… Creak. Maria, isn't that what a rope might sound like, straining under its heavy load as it swung gently to and fro…

Dry mouthed, struggling to focus on the ancient, densely-packed print, she read on. There was a short biography, mostly concerning Susannah's late husband whose glorious service to queen and country had come to a violent close in the mountains of Afghanistan.

Five years after her bereavement, Susannah Gemling had moved from Devonshire to Dalton Street, where she hid herself away for the remainder of her short life. A single Victorian woman, travelling three hundred miles to start a new life, alone in a strange town? Unusual behaviour for a gentlewoman of that era, surely.

Unless she was running away.

But from what? *Oh come on*, Maria chided herself, what was the worst situation a 19th Century lady could find herself in?

Time running out, Maria searched for further references to the tragedy. There wasn't much; perhaps the 19th Century public's attention span was no longer than its 21st Century equivalent. Then she found something, a week or so after the event. There was a suicide note. It was quoted in full and it turned Maria's soul to ice.

"I have fled a terrible darkness, but that darkness will seek me out. I thought him charming, a man of good intentions, perhaps even a balm to a widow's loneliness. But he made use of me, and left me with child. The child I should hate, but a child is a woman's, no matter the father. I must protect her. I must stand guard over her for ever."

…a child is a woman's, no matter the father…

Dizzy with shock, Maria re-read the words, hearing them in Bethany's grotesque, strangled voice.

Maria re-checked all the newspaper reports. There was nothing to indicate that Susannah had been *obviously* pregnant when she died. Surely a sensationalist rag like this one would have mentioned the fact. Or would 19th Century sensibilities overrule circulation pressure?

What if Susannah wasn't pregnant? What if the baby had already been born? A daughter she had vowed to stand guard over forever.

For ever.

Eternity.

No...She couldn't allow herself to believe... But what if it was, God forbid, true? What if she *could* cure Robert Weatherly's "phobia" and save her career, her child's future? Her own sanity?

Or was she too afraid?

~

It was almost four-thirty when Maria parked her Fiesta on the drive to Number 10 Dalton Street. She had phoned in sick then visited a DIY warehouse on the way. Now, she sat behind the wheel, wondering if she had gone insane.

Abruptly she got out, opened the Fiesta's rear hatch and retrieved her purchases: a torch, hammer, chisel and spade. She also stuffed a plastic carrier bag into her coat pocket.

The house was a shapeless mass against the night dark, a black hole that seemed to swallow Maria's soul even before she crossed its threshold. Her breath shallowed, blood roared in her ears. Cars rushed by; close, yet removed from this reality.

Quickly and as quietly as she could, Maria crossed to the front door.

Where the shaking became uncontrollable. Where pushing the key into the lock was a task too vast for her to accomplish. *Things* awaited her in there. Oh such things...

The key turned, the door swung open. She reached for the switch and that wan, yellow light splashed the mouldering walls and rubbish-strewn floor. Then it flicked out. Power failure. Oh God, why now?

And why *not* now? She wasn't welcome here. Her work was terrible work. She flicked on the torch. Its disc of yellow-white pushed back the dark, but it also created a borderland of solid night. The night pressed in, a-squirm with horrors.

In my mind, Maria told herself. *In-My-Mind!*

She shone the light carefully up the stairs, swept it over the empty steps and the age-greened statuettes. She gathered her shredded courage, closed the front door and set off for the kitchen.

The cellar entrance was in the kitchen.

The creaking began, distant, muffled.

She reached the kitchen door, which was closed. She shivered, breathing hard, wanting to turn round, to pierce the roiling darkness that pressed into the back of her head.

The kitchen then, her entrance preceded by the desperate probing of her torch. Shadows scattered, leaving behind the sink, the ancient cupboards, the smell of drains and mould.

Creak... Creak...

Louder now, no possibility that it was the aches and pains of an old house.

And there was the cellar door.

She opened it, boldly, and shone the torch down the steep stone steps, compressing the blackness into a seething, impenetrable mass at the bottom. Dear God, she could not go down there. No one could go down there.

But down she went, step by careful step. The temperature, already low, plummeted even further, slithering through the coat and thick, woollen roll-neck Maria had chosen that morning – because she had known, hadn't she, that she would end up...

Creak... Creak...

Something stirred the freezing air...

Maria suppressed a cry as the torch-disk unveiled an object on the floor of the cellar. Panicked, she bounced the light away, steadied herself, then brought the beam back round to see—

A kitchen chair, on its side, dark stained, dust-greyed, lying as if it had been thrown aside. You would stand on a chair, wouldn't you, then kick it away.

Creak... Creak...

She edged forward, joints too stiffened by dread to move quickly even if she had wanted to. She reached the bottom and shuffled towards the chair. She dropped the spade, the sound a loud, metallic clatter.

The chair was cold, slightly damp, sticky almost, and as loathsome as dead flesh. The wood crumbled under her fingers. Maria pushed it with disgusted violence. It slid a few feet away from her and came to rest at the borders of the torchlight, where it threw an immense, arachnid shadow over the cellar's dank brick wall.

The chair had left its impression etched into the dust that powdered the roughly slabbed floor. This was the spot then, which meant that directly above her...

She wanted to look up, oh how she needed to look up, straight into the heart of that relentless death-rhythm.

Maria laid the torch on the slabs, spilling a smaller cone of light onto the area of floor she wanted to work on. She picked up the spade and carefully jammed the blade into the joint between two of the slabs bearing the chair's imprint. The spade wouldn't penetrate very far, and when she levered, it popped out and sent her stumbling back. She caught her breath, then, never looking up, moved back to where the gentle breeze tousled her hair, and tried again. This time she put her shoe on the top edge of the blade, bore down with all her strength and felt the spade sink a fraction. She levered again and there was weight. She grunted and strained.

Creak... Creak... Louder... somehow frantic... and so, so close, so solid and real.

The slab tipped upwards. Maria crouched quickly, caught its icy, roughened edge then, with both hands, pitched it onto its back to reveal hard-packed soil.

Another slab, easier now, because she could slide the blade straight under. A third. She worked quickly, her back ached, her head pounded, sweat froze on her face. Her exhalations drifted like smoke through the torch beam.

Creak... Creak... bouncing dully off the mouldering walls. Creak... Creak...

The fourth slab bared the patch of earth to about two feet square. Maria caught her breath, then lifted the spade and plunged it into the ground—

The creaking stopped.

Whimpering with fright, Maria fumbled the torch from the floor and darted its light about the cellar; upturned slabs, excavated earth, the chair, and above her – she lowered the beam; she must *not* look up there.

Maria dug, hacking at the dirt, grunting in time with each blow, levering soil and dumping it on the slabs. She saw... an object, stopped and crouched to examine the tiny, yellowed shape.

It was a bone, mouldered with age. Trying to ignore the white silence that blasted out of the darkness on all sides of her, Maria scraped at the cold soil with her hands until she found a second bone, and another. Then a rib cage, attached to a minute spine, all bent into a tight foetal arc. And a skull, so small. Maria's eyes welled, she must have been premature – perhaps stillborn. Maria gently placed each piece into the carrier bag she had drawn from her coat pocket.

"...A CHILD IS A WOMAN'S, NO MATTER THE FATHER."

Something dropped onto Maria's head. A mass, like cobwebs, like *clothes*, turning to dust as they cascaded over her. She shrieked in terror and threw herself backwards, beating at her face, spitting and gagging. She crouched for a moment, sobbing, afraid to move.

Then lunged for the stairs. Only the lower steps were illuminated by the torch, which she had left behind on the floor. She lurched quickly out of the cone of light, slipped onto her hands and knees, scrambled upwards... upwards.

It was behind her, oh yes, she could feel it, could *see* it; its ancient clothing, its flesh, all gone to dust.

Out, crashing into the kitchen, bruising herself against cupboards, stumbling and staggering, then finding the open door and plunging into the lightless hallway. Her fingers brushed dank and mouldering plaster. Not far now, surely, not far. The darkness crushed her eyes, filled her mind, buffeted her senses into confusion.

And behind her, closing fast, an ice-edged tornado of despair and hate.

She blundered against the front door, bounced back, stunned, then recovered enough to claw for the handle. Found it, heavy though, and stiff. Wouldn't move, wouldn't budge.

Then there was orange street-glow, raked by wind-stirred branches, polluted by crazed shadows, but light. Oh God, light. She careered out onto the drive, raced for her car, feet crunched gravel, lungs burned. A terrible scream erupted from the house. She stumbled to a halt, looked back and saw something in the open doorway. A figure, white and wild-haired, rags of cloth and flesh fluttering about its scarecrow body. And its face. Sweet Jesus, its *face*.

Maria ran to the Fiesta, sobbing as she fumbled keys. She scrabbled them at the ignition, begged the engine to start, begged and cried out to a God she had not prayed to since she was a child. There was a throaty roar, a crunch of gears and she was reversing erratically towards the gateway. The car exploded out onto the street, headlights blinded her, a horn blared then there was only red-lit darkness.

And the road.

And that scream, reverberating through her skull, clutching her heart, piercing her soul...

"I'd managed to keep the bones," Maria said quietly. "Though God knows how. I drove way out into the countryside and parked in a gateway with my headlamps shining into a field. I had a can of petrol in the boot."

I could see her, trekking awkwardly through the heavy, ploughed soil, following the beams of the headlights to their limit, then crouching down, heedless of her clothes. The rain-edged wind plucked at her hair, wasted a dozen or so matches, until, at last, the petrol-drenched bag erupted into a brief flare of oily light.

"I heard something," she said. "It sounded lost... and angry."

"The wind," I offered, weakly.

She shook her head. "She's out there, coming for us, for..."

With a suddenness that startled me, Maria crossed to the bed and dropped to her knees by her daughter. She grasped her tiny hand and brought it to her lips. Bethany stirred, but didn't wake.

"Go away," Maria said. "Please. You can't help us. No one can."

I think I managed a strangled "But..." Then I was closing the door to her room, wondering why I wasn't going to call a doctor, what I was going to write in my report. I started down the stairs, then stopped, sure I had heard something; a steady, rhythmic creak perhaps?

Gone. Just the aches and pains of an old building.

My flesh crawling, I zipped up my coat against the sudden, vicious cold, and hurried on my way.

THE HIGGINS TECHNIQUE

Geoff

I make stories. For men, mostly. Films, photo-strips. I'm sick of the crap I produce. I want to change it. What to? Something worthy? Art? That's a fucking laugh. This contract is for the same old shite. Money, that's what matters to the nasty gentlemen who've hired me, getting the punters to enter their credit card details so they can sit all alone in front of their computer screens and wank their fucking brains out.

Tonight I had to interview a new model. It doesn't happen very often. The people I work for usually send me the women I'm supposed to use. I worry about how young some of them are. I worry about the bruises and needle tracks on their arms and ankles. I worry about where they actually come from. Half of them don't speak English, I'll bet most of them don't have a UK Passport and sailed in via Dover or Felixstowe on the Luxury Container Line. But, every now and then, someone answers the Call for Models ad on the websites I feed my work into.

My work, another fucking joke.

Usually they're not suitable, they're too nice or too stupid. They couldn't, and wouldn't, put up with what they have to do for me. They see it as an easy way into the world of modelling. Easy, it is not. This one though. I don't know what to make of her. MaryAnn (yeah, that's how you spell it) thinks I should leave well alone. As we sat there in the snug at the Hammer and Nails, I could feel her dislike of the woman, feel claws unsheathed. Although why MaryAnn should be jealous is beyond me. We're not lovers, she works for me, looks after the girls, gives them a slap when needed and a hug when it all gets too much for the little dears. But we stay out of each other's underwear. It's a professional relationship. Not that MaryAnn isn't screwable, Christ, she looks pretty good for forty-eight, a bit lined and hard around the edges but those Ava Gardner cheekbones and those dark, dark eyes of hers can still do a lot of damage.

The woman said her name was Emerald Stone. Yeah, right. She had red hair and green eyes. Her skin was pale and she looked delicate somehow. She must've been in her early thirties, and gorgeous. Not in the usual air-head way, no, she was... I don't know, interesting, yeah that's the word. Which made the rest of it wrong. Her make-up, smeared on with a trowel, panda eyes, false lashes, blood-red lipstick. And her clothes, a fluffy sweater with a vee-neck so low it was the most pointless article of clothing I've seen in my life and a skirt so short I thought she had forgotten to put one on before leaving home. There was a fur on the seat beside her, fake and cheap. She was like a caricature, everyone's idea of a porn model. When she opened her mouth, out came a load of fake estuary, which slipped every now and then to reveal something softer, though far from upper class.

When the interview was over, and the woman on her way, MaryAnn told me that Emerald Stone, so-called, must be a police officer. I told her not to be so fucking stupid. Undercover would mean a crash diet for that scrawny, wasted look, forced sleeplessness just to finish off the eyes and perfect the wan complexion, it would even mean a trip to the police doctor for some needle-mark tattoos. The accent would be right, the slang unforced. The clothes downbeat; scruffy, tee-shirts, short skirts and big boots. They would not present us with a female Lionel Blair lookalike. An exaggeration, by the way, she was still pretty fine, despite the Polyfilla and pantomime whore-wear.

"Don't go near her," said MaryAnn. "Take the girls they send you, play it safe."

She was right, of course, she's always right. But I couldn't help myself. It's the boredom I think; the crushing, pointless, sordid sameness of it all. This woman is different, a mystery, and perhaps, just perhaps, she'll help me create something I can get excited about.

Emma

Okay, first entry, audio diary of a what? A desperate woman I suppose. This had better work. I'm scared shitless but if Jack Higgins could do it, could take a boat out onto the cold, cold ocean then throw himself in to feel what it was really like then so can I.

I write. But I can't write what I don't feel. Jack Higgins told the story of the boat trip on a *Wogan* chat show. I never forgot it, because I know why he did it. I call it the Higgins Technique and it's taken me to some strange places.

But this time the water is deadly cold. I'm in a bedroom in a house somewhere outside Barnet. I've only be here for a few hours and I've already been working, that's what they call it, working. I'm shaking; I feel, grubby and disorientated. It's hard to believe that I'm actually here. I thought I'd blown it. They always say dress the part when attending a job interview, well I did. Jesus, I must have looked ridiculous, like a blow-up doll. Odd sort of interview mind you, no one said what the job actually was, but we all knew.

The woman, she calls herself MaryAnn, didn't like me. She sat and glared at me and said not a word. I felt as though she wanted to empty her Southern Comfort in my face. The man, Geoff apparently, was friendly enough, gruff, rough-edged and hard-eyed, but affable and considerate. He's stocky, but not flabby, hides his baldness with a head-shave and comes across as a cheeky chappy, a sort of Bob Hoskins, gangster-with-a-heart. I went through the motions, tried my best and left the pub planning how I would do better next time.

Geoff phoned me in the morning and suddenly it was on and I was terrified and I still am.

"Oh and drop the accent love," he said. "I don't need to know who you are or why you're doing this but perhaps you should just be yourself, yeah?"

Yeah... I mean, yes. MaryAnn came for me at about five-thirty this evening. I was in the Kilburn bedsitter I've rented for the part. It serves two purposes: one it's the kind of place a woman like Emerald Stone would live and two, there's no way I want these people to know my real address.

"You ready?" MaryAnn asked. She looks life-beaten but beautiful. There's a sort of aging hippyness to her, the way she has her thick, black (dyed?) hair, her clothes, the bangles clinking on her arms. There's film star as well. She reminds me of some Hollywood goddess of the forties or fifties.

I nodded in answer to her question, and felt like a non-speaking extra, but my mouth was too dry to trust for speech. So, suitcase in hand, and charity shop faux fur draped over shoulders made bare by my tiny, too small black dress, I locked the door of my room and led the way along the badly-lit landing. Muse accompanied us down the curving, ill-lit staircase. Even though the song's finer points were muffled by sheer volume, I recognised "Stockholm Syndrome". I like Muse, but I prefer to listen to them in the privacy of my own room, not have them blasted into my consciousness by some thoughtless bastard who believes that his musical tastes should be shared by the whole world.

The coat didn't have any buttons so I had to pull it tight about myself to keep out the December cold. A bitter east wind slapped at my legs and dug through the false fur and useless dress until it found skin and bone. MaryAnn took me to an illegally parked BMW sports convertible, thankfully with its soft-top up. She opened the door for me, but offered no smile or word. The leather seats were low and not entirely comfortable. My coat tangled about me under the seatbelt. The radio, loud with some techno-dance-trance-whatever, was quickly muted so MaryAnn could speak as we drove.

"Just do as you're told," she said. "You're an unknown. You have to prove yourself. Geoff likes his models to have a track record, likes to be able to look at their work before deciding whether or not to use them. He invests a lot of energy in these shoots. They're specialist stuff, only certain girls can cope with it. Some of them get scared and the whole thing turns into a fucking waste of time and Geoff gets pissed off. You don't want to piss him off, believe you me."

We found and followed the A1 out past Apex Corner, then left it soon after. I thought we were travelling back into Barnet, but instead we headed into the countryside. It was bloody dark out there. I'm a towngirl, I like light, any light; darkness makes my flesh crawl, darkness is like grave soil. Hedgerows flashed past, grey-stark in the headlights, caught-lost-caught-lost. A few cars blazed at us from around hidden bends then bled away behind us. Not many though. Not enough.

Suddenly there was a driveway and a run-down looking cottage. Light glowed from behind its curtained upstairs windows. The ground floor was in darkness. Adjacent to the cottage was a barn and when MaryAnn sounded the horn the barn doors were opened. A light went on. We drove inside. By the time I was out of the car, the barn doors had been closed and bolted by a tall bearded and ponytailed man.

When we went upstairs, to the studio as they call it, I discovered that the bearded man is Billy the cameraman. He isn't very friendly. In fact he hasn't spoken to me at all since I got here. I suppose I'm just another lump of meat for him to photograph.

The cottage is okay. It's clean and warm. The kitchen, like the rest of the house, is very 1970s. The studio (once the master bedroom) however, is painted bland magnolia and is cramped, crowded and made hot by the stark photographic lights. There's a double bed, covered by a new-looking duvet.

"About fucking time." Geoff was sprawled in a cheap-looking Director's chair. Suddenly the gangster had no heart. "Time to talk cash," he said. "We'll give you a grand for three days' work."

"Sounds okay."

"Too bad if it isn't. You'll fucking earn it. We're doing stills, a photo-strip, yeah? We'll call it Emerald's Torment. I want Part One up on the web tonight. We'll finish on a cliff-hanger so the wankers will be desperate to come back for more tomorrow. Okay let's make a start. Leave the coat on."

Geoff

She bothers me. She does it well, after a wooden kind of start; hands to mouth, wide-open eyes, struggling and screaming. Good set of pics. Same old story though. Same fucking old story. I think I could make something different with her. A real film. She understands. She created a story out of the same old shite, she felt the story. She bothers me.

Emma

"It doesn't sell anymore, Emma," said Caroline, my agent. "I'm sorry."

"So what do you suggest? Chick lit? Another bloody serial killer taunting another bloody cop? The Tracy Emin Code? Oh, there's always ghost-writing. There must be some ten-year old X-Factor winner out there who hasn't had their autobiography published yet."

"Emma, you know as well as I do that literary fiction just isn't moving at the moment—"

"Moving? Oh yeah, I forgot, we don't write books anymore, we manufacture units. Units that have to move."

There's a plate of food in front of me, uncooked steak, the latest fad from New York apparently, with a salmonella-flavoured raw egg. Oddly enough I've lost my appetite. Caroline is glancing around the restaurant, embarrassed by my too-loud, unreasonable anger.

"Basically Emma, yes, books are units and we do have to move them because publishing is a business." She softens. "It'll change, it always does. Books are like fashion, they come and go then come back again."

"So what is moving at the moment?"

I feel like crying. Perhaps I should switch the Dictaphone off – no, crying is part of the deal, part of the feeling. And why do I want to cry anyway? Come on, the real reason Em. Is it really the humiliation? The degradation? Think about it, pick it open, gouge it out. I have to know. I can't write without knowing.

Lilly…

No, don't go there. Come on, the room, this room.

Fuck the room…

This room, *my* room for the duration. Small bedroom, mould around the windows, dingy curtains, light bulb with no shade. The bed seems clean though. There's a bedside cabinet, some bland piece of tat from Ikea or somesuch. It's even en-suite, though the bathroom is tiny; shower, basin, mirror, a selection of cheap toiletries and a jumble of make-up. Some of it is half used, by the last woman to stay here I suppose. The skin-and-bone blonde? The raven-haired goth? I've seen them, on the Dirty Trix website, empty-eyed, wasted, going through motions and trying to convince the observer that the motions are glorious and terrifying all at the same time. Pleasure or pain, pleasure and pain?

So what did they do to me in there? Can it be crushed into vowels and consonants?

Lilly, I'm sorry...

I sat on that bed, shaking so bad I could hardly move. The bedroom/film studio, whatever they call it, reeked of maleness, the worst kind, uncaring, sweat-hard and brutal. I couldn't cry out or speak or run and that was a revelation in itself; if this had been real, I would've just sat, frozen, waiting for it to happen to me.

It was Geoff who snapped me out of it. "Fucking scream, come on, some bloke's just broken into your bedroom, wants your flesh. He might have a knife. What are you going to do, make him a cup of tea?"

I struck a pose, slowly, awkwardly. I opened my mouth the way Skin-and-Bones and Goth-Girl had opened theirs and let out a hoarse, unconvincing squeak. Geoff scowled at me but nodded to Billy to press the shutter button. I flinched back, raising a hand to protect my face, silent movie style. My arm was heavy, it ached. I could barely lift it. I smelled charity-shop mustiness, stale perfume and a hint of cigarettes in the sleeve of the fake fur – and why the hell would I be wearing my fur while sitting on my bed anyway?

Snap, snap, snap went the camera, the sound as fake as my coat, an electronic approximation, a pretend shutter like the smell they put in odourless natural gas.

"Okay, okay, take a break."

Geoff crossed to Billy who showed him the photographs, presumably scrolling them across the screen on the back of the camera.

Geoff grunted. "Emerald, try to relax, yeah? We're all friends here. Try to imagine this is real and that Paulie—" he was leaning against the wall behind the camera, tall, skinny, dressed in rapist-black, complete with balaclava "— really is coming to get you and hurt you. I mean, really hurt you."

Was he? I looked at him, and he stared back at me through the balaclava eye-holes. His eyes were dead. Blank. God, I've never seen such soulless detachment, like someone who could do anything and not think twice about it.

I nodded then forced myself to say yes. My voice was hoarse again. I swallowed, not easy when there's nothing to swallow.

"Yes." Louder this time.

Geoff sighed and went back to his Director's chair. Scream (not bad), snap-snap-snap. Cower, snap-snap-snap. Arm over my face, snap-snap-snap. Then Paulie moved in. He smelled too, mustn't forget that. He smelled of aftershave, sweat, and something animal. He grabbed my hair. Jesus he moved fast. He touched me, he grabbed my hair, he meted out violence. No one has ever done that to me, no one, ever. It was terrible, terrifying, it was a car crash that shattered everything inside me.

He *touched* me.

"Good," said Geoff. "Stay like that for a moment. Billy, see if you can get that from a few other angles."

Billy picked up a second, portable camera. And there I sat, looking up into Paulie's corpse-flat eyes, his hand in my hair, firm but not painful, the grip of an expert in fake abuse. He blinked and swallowed. My neck ached. The camera worked.

"Bit further back," Geoff growled, God, he sounded bored. "Em, put your head further back, that's it."

Me? I have to put my own head further back? What sort of assault is this?

"Okay, down onto the bed now, just lay back, that's it. Paulie, crawl onto her...stop, stop. MaryAnn, sort her leg out will you, and she's lost a shoe. Okay, Paulie get your cock out. Oh for fuck's sake Em, scream, come on, make some noise..."

Yes, he got his cock out and it was big and veiny and all the usual, but he didn't put it into me. My knickers stayed in place, hidden by my carefully arranged legs. Everything was carefully arranged, the way my skirt rode up over my thighs, my messed-up hair. Apparently I fake a good orgasm.

Geoff

Cut off her head and put on a thousand others and it's just the fucking same. But the pictures look nice and I suppose that's what the punters want. Nice clear pictures of rape and suffering. This Billy is a killer with a camera.

I wasn't sure about him when he arrived, too surly for my liking. I wanted one of my own lads, Tom or Ced, blokes I can trust to do the business, but my employers, whoever the fuck they are, wanted their man Billy, so Billy it was.

What the hell am I doing? Smoking a joint and drinking whisky at this present moment. Very funny.

Where did this start? I wanted to make films, to write scripts and screenplays. Okay, so I do that now, but it isn't art is it? Just licking and shoving and stroking and biting and now slapping and punching and strangling as well. It's And's fault. That's And, short for Andy, short for Andrew, which is short for fuck knows what, Andronicus?

I met him at an amateur filmmakers convention in Brighton. He was talent-spotting, or so he claimed. He was dressed sharp, all charm and ooze, even had some pretty bloody smart looking business cards. He watched one of my short horror flicks. No zombies or vampires, but psychological drama, a story, the terror in the imagination of the beholder. I was twenty-five, already wondering if it was too late.

"I can get you work," And said. "It may not be exactly what you want but it's a start. I mean, Michael Reeves made 'adult' films before he created *Witchfinder General*."

"So it's porn," I said.

"Glamour work, Geoffrey, specialist films. Artistic."

It was a start, or so I thought. I believed I could make artistic porn, muck with filmic integrity. Fat chance, but at least I made money, lots of it, and the work kept on coming.

I tried to make the back stories interesting. But in the end it came down to visitor/workman/neighbour, attraction and clothes off – or on in some cases, uniform and leather on.

I managed to shut my ears to the voices yammering away in my head. I tried to drown it out in real filth; animals, strangulation fetish, shit fetish. Like I said, the money was good, the "actors", willing to do anything to get work, even this sort of work, so what the hell was I worrying about? I became known as the filmmaker who didn't care what he filmed. I have a saying, entertain the Devil and he'll return the favour. Well he did.

My work came to the attention of some very dangerous people. Porn always dances round the borders of the law. What's acceptable and what isn't seems to depend on the whim of the police or some ancient old judge. Suddenly, however, there was no doubt about where I was.

But the money.

Fuck me.

All I had to do was take photos and make short films for internet download and the readies came rolling home. As long as I didn't think about what I was seeing through the lens, the heroin-addicted women submitting themselves to humiliation and violence, the obese, the skeletal, the dogs and kids.

But something was dying. I tried to blot the stink of my own shrivelled, rotting soul out of my nostrils. I drank, I sniffed and popped and injected but the smell wouldn't go away. That sort of medicine costs a lot of money and it really fucks up your creative juices.

Just as quickly as I struck gold – a grubby sort of gold I grant you, but gold nonetheless – I fucked it up and the work stopped coming my way. I was probably too difficult and unreliable to work with. The people putting the money up are not the sort of people who want to piss around with temperamental, permanently stoned prima-fucking-donnas like me. So this is redemption time, a last chance by all accounts. That's probably why MaryAnn is being so bloody pissy about everything, Nice to know she cares.

The job is relatively soft, conventional, brightly coloured and mildly rough, par for the Dirty Trix course. It's called a Damsel in Distress site, relatively mild stuff, not one of your BDSM torture sites. Now they are a challenge; well, they were once.

I never see the money men. They have a go-between for the sordid business of communing with sick bastards like me. He's a fat, shaven-headed fucker who calls himself John but talks like a Yuri or Sergei. He smiles a lot and tells me what a great artist I am.

Emma

My first whole day. I think it's Tuesday.

Why am I here?

Because of the Higgins Technique, boat-and-icy sea.

Why am I here? Because good writing doesn't sell. Because difficult doesn't sell. Because literary art doesn't sell. Because I want to rub their (my readers or my publishers?) noses in what the great book-buying public apparently want; sex and pain and damsels in savage distress.

I went into WHSmith's when I walked out on Caroline and that plate of oh-so-trendy raw steak mince and raw eggs. I pored over their bestseller shelves and tried to work it out.

I have to write. Do you understand that? If I don't write I start to think dark thoughts studded with razor blades and dead babies. Writing is a shield that deflects everything from myself, my soul, the inner, rotten, dissolving core of me.

The books I saw in Smith's made me tired. I have no desire to research police procedure or explore war torn London where feisty young women fall in love with brave, square-jawed servicemen; I'm not interested in glamour or the film industry or the music industry. Who cares which vampire is in love with which werewolf? And I can't write from a child's perspective, because my child...

Lilly, that was her name.

Other books.

Up there on the top shelf, slim volumes, monochrome covers decorated with semi-naked feminine curves and in some cases leather cuffs and gleaming chains. They have titles like *Captives of Sin* and *Slave Den*. I grabbed a handful, I don't know why, reaction perhaps. You want trash, I'll give you trash.

I blushed when I paid the pleasant middle-aged lady on the till. She pointedly ignored the books themselves, dropped them into a branded plastic bag, asked me to enter my PIN then smiled and bid me good day.

Erotica, that's what those pulp-sized novels were apparently. I'd heard of them, of course, but had never actually read any. Some of it was very good, some of it abysmal. Most of the titles I picked up were sadomasochistic in a soft-focus, afternoon TV movie sort of way. They involved women in some sort of captivity, often at a fantastical gothic academy or harem where they learned the arts of seduction under the strict tutelage of some fearsome dominatrix. Disobedience and failure were punished thoroughly (though seldom with any blood being spilt, these were not the works of the Marquis) and detailed and explicit descriptions of these punishments seemed to form the main meat of the narrative.

The heroines, who seemed to be semi-willing, always innocent, unsure and afraid, derived an odd sensual enjoyment from their trials and tribulations.

Aha. You want moveable units, Caroline, you'll get moveable units. But there can be no writing without application of the Higgins Technique. I was fairly certain the training centres described in the books didn't exist, so where was my boat and cold ocean? The internet of course, God bless it. Where would we be without its infinite helpfulness?

I filled the search engine box with such words as "punishment", "bondage" and "training". Yes, I was shocked by some of it and not convinced that all the girls were acting. It didn't take long for me to feel stained and depressed by the parade of images, women, always women, brutalised, humiliated and degraded. Why the hell did these people allow themselves to be displayed like this? What the fuck was going on here?

It took a while to translate the patois. "Call for Models" was apparently what I was looking for.

So, now it's Tuesday and I'm a *Captive of Sin* and it's raining outside the *Slave Den*. The room is warm though and the bed surprisingly comfortable. No one has called me, no one told me what time I'm supposed to make an appearance. Perhaps I should just wait. Which allows me to think.

Lilly...

There is no Lilly. Lilly is gone. I am gone. This is the shell, the hard outer coating that was left when the soft insides dissolved away. What do I feel?

It is dull grey, soundtracked by the rain beating at the window. Will they beat me? I'm shaking a little, my stomach is clenched and my bowels are filling up. My heart is beating fast, not hammering, thundering or pounding, just beating fast enough to make me breathless. I am afraid. Will they let me go home when this is finished? That thought is a bad one. I don't know these people. As far as they are concerned I am little Miss Alonesome. No one will miss me. I know too much...

Oh God, help me. I can't swallow, I can't move.

Okay, okay, I have to calm down. They are not going to kill me. They are going to make me do horrible degrading things then pay me and send me on my way. Let's think about fear. What is it like? Physical, a weight on my chest, my joints and muscles ache from tension, I feel as if I have flu, my skin is sensitive and sore. My mind is in a...whirl, corny, poor choice of cliché, but a true one. It won't stop working, it spins and creates images and scenarios, half-formed, smoky horrors. The whole thing roars, on and on. Someone's knocking at the door. Jesus switch off, where's that bloody off button, Jesus, Je—

It was MaryAnn. She brought me coffee and toast and told me, snapped at me in fact, to be up and in the studio at eleven. I am to wear the same clothes as last night. She has brought some new underwear, all black lace and silkiness and still in the wrapper. A sequel then. The further perils of Emerald Stone.

Geoff looked ill, white-faced. He smelled unwashed and the stink of him made me feel sick. When he lifted his coffee mug to his lips I noticed that he was shaking. So was I. On time though, dead on eleven, made up, fragrant and stifling in the dress and fur coat.

"You ready Em?" Geoff growled.

"Yes." Was I?

"Good girl. Today's epic then. That bastard who assaulted you last night has kidnapped you and brought you back to his lair to have his wicked way with you."

"Is that it?" I asked.

"What do you mean is that it?"

"Well..."

He sat back and I assumed that he meant for me to go on.

"Well, does she try to escape, or fight back?"

"Fucked if I know," he said and laughed his wheezy cigarette drenched laugh.

"Sorry, but, well, tell me if it's none of my business but can't we create a story out of this?"

He sat forward, suddenly, and glared at me with bloodshot eyes. "You're right," he said. "It isn't any of your fucking business. Now, stand over there by the door. Paulie, grab her arm. Em, put your hands behind you back and pretend you're tied up." I did as I was told, struggling as best I could without giving the game away. It was difficult not to use my hands for balance.

Geoff was irritable. He made us repose some of the shots two, three, even four times. I was overacting, underacting, he could see my hands.

Paulie's grip was tight. He said nothing, didn't look at me even when he had his hands round my neck and was staring into my face. His eyes were locked onto mine but the creature inside was asleep, or looking elsewhere.

The entrance completed, I was ordered to sit in a straight-backed chair in the middle of the bedroom. This time the tying-up was real. MaryAnn did the work though Paulie would step in every so often to pose over the knots. MaryAnn was not gentle and when she had finished my wrists and arms were twisted up and crushed against the back of the chair and my ankles brutally cinched against the two front legs.

Paulie went through the motions. He kissed me, no tongues, his mouth a mint-breathed, fleshy hole. He grabbed my hair for a couple of photographs then faked a slap complete with my own dramatic swing of the head.

Do I sound bored? There I was bound and helpless and I'm talking about it as though it's just another day at the office. Perhaps bored isn't the right word. Being trussed to the chair drove me to the edge of panic, I felt claustrophobic, I wanted my arms free, I wanted to be able to fight back if things got too rough, I wanted to be able to move.

And why is it supposed to be sexy anyway? I'm bent up, awkward, my knees forced together by the way my ankles are tied to the chair legs, like some gangling, toe-turned pre-adolescent. I felt foolish, humiliated. I was surprised when the others didn't laugh at me. And then there's the discomfort, the abrasions and aches. It must be bad for you to be held in one position for so long, circulation slowed by rope-crushed blood vessels.

Geoff's mood, edgy at the start of the shoot, turned progressively fouler. Halfway through, he instructed MaryAnn to "mess me up". For a moment I thought he meant for her to beat me or cut me, but instead, she untied my hands, wrenched the coat off my shoulders, unzipped the back of my dress and pulled it all down to expose some flesh. When she re-tied my hands Geoff shouted at her to "Make the fucking knots exactly the same as they were last time. Christ, haven't you heard of continuity?"

In an odd sort of way it made the exposure of my breasts a little more bearable because the focus was not on me but on doing Geoff's bidding and trying to keep him sweet.

As for me, I felt cold; I shivered despite the stifling heat of full-blast radiators and photographic lights. These were my breasts, they belonged to no one else, they are private, yet there I was allowing them to be displayed to these strangers and then to a million other strangers on the internet where they would provide friction for a thousand, hand-driven flesh-pumps. No one said *phwoarrr*. No one licked dry lips or drooled. Paulie grabbed them and pretended to bite them. Then out came his cock so he could pretend to do a deed, impossible in real life, but I groaned and moaned and pulled the right expressions and Geoff seemed satisfied.

"Was that enough story for you?" Geoff growled at me when it was done and I was rubbing cream into my rope burns. "Did you find your motivation? Huh? Layer upon layer of meaning and sub-text?"

"Sub-sex more like," Billy said and everyone chuckled, except me.

MaryAnn brought sandwiches and coffee then we were off again and this time I was down to my underwear, shoes on of course. I mean, what self-respecting kidnap victim would take off her heels when she was chained and gagged and thrown onto a bed like a partygoer's coat?

So what sort of book is this going to be? Erotica, that's why I'm here, isn't it? The Higgins Technique? Well, it isn't working. The women in those slim little books didn't complain about chafed wrists and crumpled clothing. Their captors were not chain-smoking, unshaven, BO-ridden, middle-aged men. Their chains were not rust-stained and their gags didn't taste of plastic and dried saliva, with buckles that caught strands of hair when they were tightened. They didn't see themselves as trussed and stuffed oven-ready chickens complete with pinkish-blue, goose-pimpled flesh.

An exposé then, the sordid truth behind the brightly-coloured fantasy offered by the great god internet? But would it sell, would it be a moveable unit?

Geoff

John came to see me tonight. Shame he was too early for me to be properly stoned.

"New stuff, same old stuff yes?" Didn't Khrushchev say something similar?

"I'm doing my best." How pathetic that sounded.

"We want a better story, different."

"So do I."

"Good old chap." He slapped my arm and grinned his crocodile grin. "What are your ideas?"

"I want the captive to fall for her captor. I want them to communicate and I want the woman to gain the psychological upper hand. I want Stockholm Syndrome. I want *The Collector*."

"What collector?"

"It's a film, Samantha Egger."

"Forget collectors and whatever happened in Stockholm yes? These strips look nice but they're not...exciting. She's a lovely woman. Use her."

"I am fucking using her."

"I know, I know and pretty she looks all tied-up, but is not sufficient, yes?"

"Yes, fucking yes, yes, yes. So let me untie her and make a real bloody story out of this. It can still be hot and sweaty—" I know I'm winding the bastard up and it's dangerous. I can't help myself "—but it can have a little depth."

"Yes, deeper is right. Deeper and darker. Good torture. Hurt her. Get Paulie to piss on her, I don't care, but is rare to get such a sweet-looking bird."

God save us from Russians who think they're Alfie.

"Punters, they like to see good-lookers get really hurt, yes?"

"I know, I know. I'll sort it."

"You sure you can believe in her?"

"She's doing the business so far."

"No, no, are you sure she is who she says so? We are a little worried she might be a police."

"She's not a police. Trust me."

He grinned and slapped my arm. "Of course I trust you, but be careful, yes?"

"Yes."

"And remember what Hitchcock said…"

"Torture the heroine, yes I know." Every-bloody-time.

Emma

Today I went into the dark. I can't stop shaking and crying. I don't want to talk about it. But I have to.

I was already scared before I went into the studio. I couldn't find the Dictaphone, not right away. It was in my suitcase, where it was supposed to be, but buried right at the bottom under my clothes. It should have been hidden in a pair of thick socks rolled-up in my big charcoal jumper. I thought I'd been careful about that, religious almost. I must have forgotten to conceal it properly last night. Everything else seemed okay, everything where it was supposed to be.

No one left the studio after we finished yesterday's shoot. I was even invited to stay for a drink and a tote on the communal joint. I passed it on; I can't let my guard down. I did have a drink though, but only one, vodka and coke. MaryAnn was pouring and she was as mean with the coke as she was generous with the vodka. I was exhausted and crawled back here to make my report then I must have fallen asleep straight away.

Does all this matter? I'm rambling because I'm upset. Because I'm broken into little pieces.

Okay, today.

The dark.

They wanted me naked. MaryAnn told me when she brought my coffee and toast. She left a dressing gown for me. It smelled of washing powder, thank God. I showered, barely able to move I was so scared. The dressing gown was made from a silvery-grey, faded satin material. It was cold and slithered over me when I pulled it on.

I went to the studio barefoot. Once there I kept the dressing gown on for as long as I could.

"Come on Em, you gone shy on me?" Geoff looked even worse, the tremors more pronounced. He stank of cigarettes, booze and sweat.

I fumbled the belt and struggled out of the gown. MaryAnn took it from me. And there I was, all of me, frail, pale and vulnerable. I shivered and felt awkward. I tried to hide myself with my arms and hands but it wasn't possible for long. I did not feel attractive or sexy. I felt small, weak, a mess. Images of shaven-headed, emaciated women being shoved into Nazi showers flashed through my mind, then a remembered photograph, glimpsed during a schooldays visit to the Imperial War Museum, of similarly nude women being herded over a field towards a firing squad. One had carried a baby. A baby, Lilly... I thought I was going to cry then, but managed to regain control.

They did some complicated roping first, Japanese apparently; it was excruciating and left me cross-legged on the floor, hunched forward, head bowed and shivering. Paulie waved a scarlet candle over me then drew back so that MaryAnn could smear imitation wax over my breasts. I had to writhe and scream. Writhing hurt. Screaming was easy.

All the time their faces were bland and bored. It was degradation by numbers. And, astonishingly, I became bored too, fed up with laying there unable to move, with being folded and twisted and pulled about.

They made me crawl along on my hands and knees, tugged by a chain and a dog collar. They made me drink water from a bowl on the floor. The room was grey and dirty and the world was grey and dirty.

But that wasn't what made me cry.

It was the cocoon.

And not even that, it was what I found in there, in the dark.

The cocoon was, essentially, a one-piece rubber sleeping bag, zipped-up at the back. Once on it fitted tight and restricted all movement. Within seconds it was hot and clammy. I lay on the bed, unable to do more than twist a little and raise my head. It was already a claustrophobic hell. Then MaryAnn pulled the matching hood over my head and zipped it in place. The hood had only two small holes for my nostrils. No other openings, no compromise or mercy. It clung to my scalp and pressed in on my face and suddenly there was immobility and utter, utter darkness. I think they strapped my arms and legs as well but by then I was lost in the screaming, roaring black, by then I was in my coffin, a million tons of earth bearing down on its fragile wooden lid, by then I was smothered by nightmare, by a panic so complete it paralysed every muscle in my body, danced on every nerve.

I wanted to move, just to bloody, fucking move. I wanted light, just a glimmer, a crack. I wanted sound, any sound other than the howl of blood through my skull. My bladder let go and I wet myself. The stink of it churned my stomach towards nausea.

Oh God, not in here, I'll choke...

Then I heard a sound. A baby, crying for me, somewhere deep in that red-dark. I wanted it to stop. But it cried on and on. I tried to move because the baby was desperate. It, she, Lilly, wanted me. Needed me. But I couldn't get to her. I tried, God I tried.

Did she cry that night?

Did she cry out to her mother, who was asleep, arms wrapped about some lover she had picked up in a club? If she did, I was too drunk and fuck-tired to hear. I had what I wanted for the night, a faceless, brainless pile of muscle and cock to assuage the loneliness left by the departure of my beloved bloody husband?

And why did he depart?

Because he was jealous of Lilly apparently, because he "couldn't handle the way I had shifted all my affection onto our daughter." *Our* daughter. *We* made her. He said that I wasn't the same, I was moody and obsessed. We didn't have any fun anymore. Surprise fucking surprise.

So he walked out and never came back.

I was lonely, for God's sake, what was I supposed to do?

Silence. I woke to it, head pounding, the walking penis's tattooed arm across my chest. Silence. She was supposed to wake me while it was still dark, demanding her five-am feed. But it was light and the time on my fumbled mobile phone was eight-twenty-three.

I remember that time. I will always remember that time. Thursday morning, 6th May, eight twenty-three.

I stumbled into the nursery, into that little room with its teddy bear wallpaper and mobiles and cot—

Blue, she's blue, her tiny mouth half open, her eyes half shut. Blue and limp and so very, very cold.

The brainless one stood around while I shrieked and howled and hugged the lifeless bundle of flesh and death that was my daughter.

She's crying now, God she's crying and crying and crying and I want it to stop – No, no I didn't mean it, no, don't stop. I don't want the silence. Not again. Jesus, please don't stop.

I writhed and struggled and I suppose that was what they wanted. I couldn't breathe, through my nose. Every inhalation pressed the rubber over my face. And the universe was roar and crying and redness. Then silence. Like the silence that morning, utter, complete, unbearable, relentless silence. *Dead* silence.

Geoff

Em's got a tape recorder hidden in her room, a digital Dictaphone. MaryAnn told me tonight, after the shoot. She was furious and more scared than I've ever seen her.

"I told you," she shouted. "I told you she was the fucking filth."

I tried to tell her that having a Dictaphone didn't mean she was a policewoman. But I couldn't make myself heard and, worse, I had no other explanation. She had survived the cocoon hadn't she? She didn't look too good when we pulled the hood off but she had stuck it out. I think I fell in love with her at that moment. Most of the girls can only take five minutes. She did twenty.

But her eyes...

What the fuck went on in there?

MaryAnn kept yelling at me to do something, but what? I don't know what to do. I should confront her, threaten her, let her know she's in the shit. But if she is a copper she's going to call in her mates straight away and that'll be it.

"Have you ever been inside?" MaryAnn seemed to have calmed down enough to actually talk to me.

No I haven't and I intend to keep it that way.

"Well it isn't all fucking Jacuzzis and colour tellies. I am never going back there, Geoff." She was crying now but she wouldn't let me give her a hug.

"I'll kill myself before I'll let anyone put me back in that shithouse."

We could make a run for it, I suppose. Put the lovely Emerald Stone in the boot and dump her somewhere. If we trussed her up we could be a long way away before she got free or anyone found her.

There is another way, of course.

No, no I can't do that. Fuck me no. Oh, I can pretend, I can tell a story, but I can't do it for real.

I need to talk to the others before I'm too pissed and stoned and tired. We're doing nothing wrong, a bit of soft porn, nothing worse than the shite they sell off the top shelf at the local newsagents. The law isn't going to be interested in a bit of play acting is it?

But what about the stuff I've done in the past? Is that what they're after? Or is it the bastards who are paying me for this? They must be making good money out of these sites, money for other business interests that might be of concern to the forces of righteousness.

But she isn't a copper, because if she is she's the clumsiest bloody bit of undercover work I've ever seen. Christ, what's the recorder for? She's making her own fucking porno site. Is that it? Stealing my ideas, robbing my creative genius? Very funny.

Christ I'm tired. One more day. Something rough and imaginative tomorrow. Food, mud, nipple clamps. I don't know. I've run out of ideas. I've had enough. *The Collector*, then, yeah – no, because the woman dies in that film. Okay, she gets free, she beats the shit out of Paulie, he beats the shit out of her, they talk, yeah, she seduces him. All distressed and ragged, she seduces him and they make fucky-fuck all weary and muddy and... I don't know. I've run out of ideas. I have to talk to the others. I have to talk to somebody.

Oh Christ, there's a car out there. Someone's called John and his nasty mates and told them about the dictaphone. Wouldn't have been MaryAnn.

Billy. It was fucking Billy. Their bloody man on the inside.

Emma

I think I found the book in the dark yesterday. It won't sell, it'll hurt. But that is the only book I can write. It won't be top-shelf erotica, in fact it won't be erotica of any kind. It will be exorcism, cleansing, confession. It'll be self-mutilation, a carving out of guilt and soul. I want to start it, now.

One more day. One more shoot. I'll grab the big and shapeless charcoal jumper and some jeans. I'll wear trainers. If they want leather corsets and rubber knickers they'll have to tell me. I'm cold and tired and I want to go home. They all had a big row last night. I could hear them downstairs, everyone shouting. I don't know how long it went on for because I fell asleep. God I'm sick of this. Better get dressed. A car's just pulled up. I'll keep the curtains drawn, stay in the dark. See nothing. It's raining again. I'm nervous and frightened and tired and bored and I want to go home and I want to burn the book out of myself. Lilly, that's its title. Okay, it's half-ten, time for a shower and some face-paint.

Romance In D Flat

1: Woman

"Thanks," I replied to the woman's praise of my harmonica playing. She was following me through the hot and crowded Jam Nite pub. I was out of breath, desperate for a beer and not really taking much notice.

"Seriously." She drew up at the bar beside me. "I mean good."

If this was going to be a conversation then it needed to be a fast one because the next act was tuning his Strat and discussing his fifteen minutes of deafening fame with the house band.

"I should be," I said as I turned to look at the woman properly. "I played for a living most of my life..." My impatience ended right there. The woman was tall with long, gleaming black hair. She wore an unseasonable fur coat, open to reveal a navy, Bardot-neckline dress and pearls at her throat. A broad-brimmed hat was dipped low over her eyes, throwing her face into shadow and deepening the mystery.

"Drink?" she asked before I could. Her voice was a purr, her accent correct and, like her clothes, somehow old fashioned.

"Guinness, Extra Cold."

She relayed the order to the fresh-faced young barman, who immediately abandoned any idea of first-come-first-served and got to work on my beer.

"And exactly what sort of music was it that earned your living?"

"Blues," I said.

I saw a smile. "Blues. Yes, that suits you."

I suppose it was because I dressed the part, a fifty-two year old man who still wore denim and kept his hair on his collar.

"So why aren't you playing professionally now?"

"Had enough of the road and the crap that goes with it." The authorised cover-story, well-practised and convincing.

Christ, where had I seen her before? And that perfume was also familiar, strong even here in this micro-world of aftershave, male deodorant and music sweat.

"I would like you to play for me," she said.

I was momentarily flustered. Her request smacked of euphemism.

"Oh yeah?" Why the hell was I being so cagey? It wasn't every night, in fact it was virtually never, that someone as gorgeous as this approached me in a bar and gave me flattery without making it sound like flattery.

"I sing, and I'm rehearsing for a charity promenade concert. The organisers are looking for something unusual to put into the repertoire. Listening to you tonight gave me an idea. There is a piece," she said. "By Vaughn Williams."

No, oh no…

"Romance in D Flat." Blurted out before I could stop myself. "Written for Larry Adler in 1951, after he challenged Williams to compose a classical work for the harmonica."

She showed no surprise that I had heard of that particular musical curiosity.

"The answer's no," I continued, shaken. "Sorry." And I was, because I wanted her very badly. "Blues, that's my music, not Vaughn Williams."

"Think about it," she said then added a "Please Martin," that tore my heart to shreds.

Because Kate used to say that.

And she was the only person who didn't call me Marty.

"What's the charity?" I didn't really want to know, but she was on her feet, body language telling me she was about to leave. I just wanted her here for a little longer.

"It supports victims of wrongful imprisonment."

The music started, Davey Tapp playing *Wishing Well*. Again. Every bloody week the same bloody song. But I wasn't listening. I was clawing my way through the pack of bodies round the bar, trying to catch the woman.

This wasn't funny, not funny at all.

I stood in the pub's open doorway, staring up and down the street; cars, people, the glow and glare of shop windows, the clatter of a train, but no glimpse of fur coat and wide-brimmed hat.

When I got back to the bar I saw a brown A4 envelope, left on her stool. My name was written neatly on the front; fine hand, black ink.

2: Romance

I opened the envelope when I got back to the cramped pre-war terrace tumbledown I called my house. As expected, it contained a music script; *Romance in D flat for harmonica, piano and strings*. The harmonica part was translated into tab form, hole numbers instead of notation; blown notes plain, drawn notes circled. Convenient, seeing as I had never learned to read music.

Twenty-five years ago Kate had begged me to play the same work.

Because *she* sang, and had been asked to perform at a charity promenade concert. Because the organisers were looking for something unusual to put into the repertoire. "Listening to you practising gave me an idea," she said. "There's a piece by Vaughn Williams..."

Kate had bought a recording and I didn't like it from the start. The Romance was redolent of something that tasted bad. It was discordant and haunting. It was like the theme of some creaky, London-set, black-and-white thriller; it was fog and seedy old pubs and seedy old men.

It was Arnold Cryer.

But I gave in as I always gave in to Kate. Who couldn't?

Her contribution was to be *Un bel dì vedremo* from *Madama Butterfly* and I knew it would steal the show. She sang so beautifully it sometimes made me cry because I could not understand why someone as lovely as her could put so much faith in a drunken, dope-addled wreck like me.

I was just about living on the road when we met, moving from band to band, not wanting to stay in one place for more than a few nights, restless and haunted.

A prog rock outfit whose name I'd long forgotten had hired Kate

Wilson to perform on some of their pretentious nonsense. It was a last ditch attempt at prog rock survival, a vain hope because, by then, even punk was being shovelled out through the back door.

There was a sound check for a one day festival. The clear grey eyes of the prog rock soprano met the bloodshot piss holes of The Blues Police's harmonicky man and something happened, something bloody miraculous. Or was it? Kate was not in great shape either. She was fragile, addicted to anti-depressants, crushed by the pressure. We were made for each other.

I stared at the manuscript, tired and on edge. It was as if no time had passed between now and the first time I saw this music. The whole thing was beyond coincidence. Suddenly there was a come-on from a woman in a pub who oozed the type of sexuality a loser like me can only dream of, and who had all-but repeated Kate's entreaty for me to play the Williams word-for-word.

Even worse, she was wearing the same perfume as Kate.

One of Arnold Bloody Cryer's descendants, out for revenge? If so, why the games, why not just confront me, throw beer in my face, slap me and get it over with? The recycle bin was the best place for this sheaf of waste paper.

I never got to play the Williams piece in that far-off charity prom. Cryer hanged himself a week before. Two nights later, beaten by my resulting breakdown (a climactic Armageddon of a breakdown), the long-suffering and eternally loyal Kate finally gave in and walked out.

This was why I had swapped The Road and rock n roll glory for Friday Jam Nites at the Black Prince in South Ruislip.

This was why I now lived in this mouldy pile of bricks and scratched a living as a shop-assistant at Sound n Light; specialists in electric music accessories.

Kate walked out and I'd never seen or heard from her since.

3: Monster

The humid summer dark ground into my eyes, stole my breath and forbade sleep.

"Please Martin." That's what Kate had said. "Think of it as an exorcism."

I sat up and pushed away the duvet? No Kate, not an exorcism. I lied to you about Cryer. I lied to everyone about him. I swung my feet from the bed and fumbled for the bedside lamp. The longer I left this, the worse it would get.

I crossed to the cheap and soulless flat-pack unit in the corner of the room and rifled through the assorted harps that filled the top drawer.

The chromatic was a gift from Kate, a bribe to get me to play the Romance. It was still in its box, a gleaming, substantial artefact, bigger than my diatonic harmonicas and much more complex to play.

I'd brought the sheet music upstairs with me. It was on the floor by the bed, not in the recycle bin. I blamed the lapse on middle-aged absent-mindedness. It wasn't, of course – my subconscious had been way ahead of me, had known that this moment was going to come.

I picked the sheet music up and smoothed it out on the duvet. A sigh, then I blew the first note, the next, another, slowly clawing my way into the piece. I was hesitant, stilted and awful. This would take a hell of a lot more effort than I felt inclined to give it.

No. I'd started this so I was going to finish; time for some exorcism blues. Out demon, out, back into your box you monster in the dark.

I played on, a little out of breath, mouth dry.

Something cold crawled over my skin. I coughed into the instrument and the tune, what there had been of it, splintered into a tumble of squeaks and squawks. The air was suddenly damp and cold. The light changed too, became diffuse. The room was growing misty. I tasted dirty moisture, smoke, ash.

Smog.

Marty?

That bloody voice, a distant, chesty rattle.

Marty, you all right boy? Practising the old mouth organ are yer?

I surged off the bed and slammed open the door. Fog rolled up the stairs, coiling into the steep, narrow space like smoke. He was down there, Arnold. His emphysema-laden gasps rattled through the house and...

...became a motorbike, hammering down the street outside, too fast and too loud.

There was no fog, only the piss-coloured landing light and the empty staircase with its vile, threadbare carpet. The front door was bolted shut.

I could still taste it though; smog, the fog-and-smoke meld that had clogged the capital's lungs back in the post-war greyness of the fifties.

4: Addict

So how was she going to contact me, this fur-coated practical joker in the blue dress with the Bardot neckline? She wasn't. The grenade had been tossed, the switch-flicked, the stable door thrown wide.

I still hated him. No amount of guilt could change that. Arnold Bloody Cryer had stolen my mother and driven my father out of my life. I don't know how because my dad was a decent man and that old bastard wasn't. Cryer was a butterfly who became a caterpillar.

I was eleven the first time mum brought him home. I hadn't seen dad for a while and she had told me, matter-of-fact, not a tear in sight, that he had deserted us. That made no sense. Like I said, he was a decent, loving man. Quiet, gentle, working hard at a place he simply called The Office to support us. He taught me to play chess, to repair a bicycle puncture, to change a fuse and to play the harmonica. Now he was gone and there was a new man on my mother's arm.

His smile was too wide and too friendly. His hair was too neat, his suit too sharp. Good looking though he was, I could see that he was older than dad had been, a man from a slightly different time. He had a broad London accent, he talked to mum quietly and with a great affection that made my skin crawl. He called her "Dawlin'".

"He knows how to show me a good time," mum said. "He's kind and exciting."

Cryer never raised a hand to me, or, as far as I know, my mother. Yet, as the façade crumbled, and the money he promised ("Got deals in the offing Marty boy, you mark my words son, this time next year we won't be living this hovel...") never materialised, my mother's devotion to him seemed to grow deeper, while her devotion to me diminished.

Cryer quickly lost the sharply defined angles of the rogue-with-a-heart charmer. He grew fat, he lost his hair, the endless cigarettes flooded his lungs with fluid, his throaty laugh and gravelled voice became a rattle and a wheeze. His relentless coughing drove spikes into my skull. Everything about him irritated, infuriated and incensed me.

"Marty, you all right boy?" he'd say when I came home from school. His voice grated, his regard for me froze my blood. I wanted him to shut up and never speak to me. "Good day mate? Going upstairs to practice the old mouth organ are you? I like listening to that. Do your homework first though."

And as confused puberty became surly, resentful adolescence I began to look for ways of getting rid of him...

Then, years later, when I first heard Adler's harmonica slithering, metallic, over Williams' gentle strings I saw the dank, smothering, smog-bound swamp from which my stepfather had crawled as the last of the capital's Blitz-fires were dampened down. I saw the pubs and the chancers and the shysters and the noisy, boozy faux-camaraderie and the jangly-piano sing-alongs and the cards and the dark-alley deals.

I saw it again last night.

Didn't I?

No, of course I didn't. I was drunk, I was exhausted. I was shaken from my encounter with Miss Sophistication. It was a dream, an LSD flashback. But that bloody piece of music was in my head now and as I endeavoured to show my third Saturday morning customer Sound n Light's extensive selection of effects pedals, I was distracted by the knowledge that the sheet music and my harmonica were still on the bed and I would have to drink away the temptation to play them again before I went home tonight.

The customer, some lad with dreams of rock stardom, walked out in the end, fed up with the pauses in my conversation and my fumbling lack of dedication to his needs. Don, the owner came over to berate me. This was Saturday, our busiest day and two customers had left Sound n Light empty-handed (Don's Unforgivable Sin) thanks to me. "What the hell's wrong with you Marty? Sort it, now, or there'll be someone else working here on Monday."

It was Don's favourite threat. I'd been working for him, selling amps and lighting rigs, for four years now, long enough not to put too much store in that near mythical other person.

Apologies of course, a fresh determination to serve the customer. I didn't do too badly. My invisible understudy would have to wait another day for his moment in the sun.

"Pint?" Don said as he locked up.

"Yeah, why not."

"Good, you can tell Uncle Don what the problem is."

I didn't, of course. We found an outside table in the beer garden at the Barrel of Monkeys and I mumbled about loneliness and being a bit depressed and he said something about understanding because one moment I had a glittering career with The Blues Police, the next it had all collapsed around my ears, so who wouldn't be feeling down now and then.

"You're right mate," I said and started on my third Speckled Hen of the night. "But it was good while it lasted."

The sun had dipped behind the surrounding buildings by then. The sky was sharp blue, the air warm and at that moment all was well with the world.

But all Saturday evenings come to an end. I wasn't inclined to sleep with Don, and no ladies had thrown themselves at us and offered invites to their beds, so I wandered home, alone. The town was brash and binge-drunk noisy. The young had claimed the remnants of the night, but they left me alone. I suppose I still looked big and mean enough to ward off trouble.

Once home, I tried the television, but it didn't help. I paced. I swigged Bells straight from the bottle and all it did was sober me up.

Then I went upstairs.

And there they were, on the bed, sheet music and chromatic harmonica, just as if someone had laid them out for me.

Exorcism, Kate said.

Atonement more like.

I sat on the floor and stared at them. The room was hot and close and I knew I should open a window but I was too tired to move.

I found myself at the wardrobe, pulling out a thick sweater and suddenly aware that I'd grabbed a leather biker jacket on my way up. I couldn't remember taking the jacket from the peg, but here I was on this sultry, sleepless night in June, pulling on my warmest winter clothes. Here I was picking up my harp and smoothing out that sheet music. Here I was blowing that first bar.

Nothing happened. And nor would it, because last night's nonsense had been just that; hallucination, dream, LSD flashback…

The temperature plummeted, the air grew damp and the harmonica was icy in my hands. I struggled on, my breath puffs of steam that curled around the instrument and merged with the cold, cold smog boiling into the room.

Marty?

Oh, there he was, that butterfly-turned-caterpillar.

You all right boy? Had a good day?

I focussed on the sheet music, which was now crutch not necessity, because I remembered all of it. The notes flowed, building, demolishing then re-forming the structures and landscapes of the piece.

Practising that old mouth organ again?

Another sound. The click of heels.

I stopped then and understood that things had changed. The floor was wrong, no longer carpet. The bed, the wardrobe, the table lamp were all gone. There was a different light, wan and diffused by the mist. The clip of heels grew louder. A figure emerged from the fog. It was a woman, the collar of her fur coat turned up, face hidden beneath a broad-brimmed hat.

5: Street

She walked past, the fog torn by her passage then swirling back to fill the vacuum. The floor was tarmac, the walls the faintly glimpsed façade of buildings and the light was a streetlamp. I set off in pursuit of the woman and saw her as a slender silhouette that swung right and disappeared round the corner of a building. The urge to follow her was strong. I didn't want to be lost here.

I saw shop windows as night-black, eyeless sockets. There was something equally as empty about the buildings themselves, as if they were frontage-only props in a film set.

The woman was briefly detailed by the glare from a solitary, bright-lit window, then she pushed open a door and went inside. There was a snatch of voices, laughter, the tinkling of a piano.

I hesitated; who, or what, was inside that place?

Oh come on, you know...

I had to go in. It was why I was here.

The pub was isolated on both sides by bombed-out ruin, vague twists of scorched rubble, softened by a combination of mist and lamplight. There would have been a lot of Blitz relics still standing in his day.

I reached for the door.

6: Pub

The first thing I noticed was the smoke, a nicotine fog that curled into every corner of the public bar. Then there were smells, too strong to be contained by the all-pervasive cigarette odour; sweat, halitosis, damp clothes. The light was dim orange, the décor all dark browns and fag-yellowed plaster.

The clientele were mostly men, although there were a few women, their faces hidden under headscarves, their bodies inside long, heavy coats. The men were bareheaded but kept cloth caps, homburgs and trilbies within reach. Hairstyles were short backs-and-sides, badly cut, Brylcream-smoothed. Those who were balding vainly disguised their lack with combed-over rakes of hair. All the men wore ties and some form of suit, most of them a little threadbare and poor-fitting. I was suddenly conscious that my sweater and biker jacket would be construed as strange, scruffy work clothes.

Talk was loud, laughter louder still, all framed by brown and neglected teeth.

Knowing that I couldn't stand here by the door for much longer, I set off towards the bar, and the woman, who was perched on a stool talking to a fellow customer. He was tall, wore glasses and sported a skilfully barbered, tightly slicked hairstyle. His suit looked to be in better condition than those of his fellow drinkers, and expensively tailored. When he caught my eye and smiled in greeting, I saw that his dentist was of a higher standard as well.

"Can I buy you a drink?" he said, all charm and affability.

"Please," I was aware that the woman was looking at me, her gaze steady, a hint of a smile on her red-glossed lips.

"Guin—" I stopped myself. There was no sign of any Guinness in here. "Brown ale."

"You heard the man," my host said to the stocky, scowling barman. He held out his hand to me. "Jim Simpson."

"Martin Andrews," I said.

The woman's smile grew more visible, but she gave no sign of recognition.

I took a chance and offered my hand to her. She accepted the greeting. Her glove-hidden grip was strong. "Rita Callan," she answered.

"Do you like it here?" Jim asked me. He took a pack of cigarettes from his jacket pocket. We both lit up.

"I'm not sure."

"Oh come on, you can be honest, you're among friends." And for a moment it certainly seemed that way; warm, roughly comfortable, a place of content and laughter.

"Convincing," I said. My pint arrived.

"Even down to the warm beer," Jim chuckled. "It's real enough, Martin. And it suits him perfectly."

"Where is he?" I felt as if I was pushing my luck.

"Here and there. Difficult to pin down is our Arnold."

"Give me a clue." I must have sounded impatient because Jim's smile faltered, as did the noisy conviviality around me. I felt Rita's hand on my arm, the contact was a warning.

"Why do you want to know?" Jim was all amiability again and the noise level rose once more.

"I need to talk to him." Was that all? How pathetic after what I had done to the man.

"You'll have to get to him first." Jim toasted me with his brandy. "And good luck."

Rita's hand was still on my arm. I glanced back at her. The smile was gone. When I looked round again, Jim had also disappeared. No sign of him, no glimpse of slicked hair and expensive suit among the demob and cheap and threadbare.

"Simpson couldn't stop me coming for you," Rita said. "He's just a Warder, a Screw. These walls, that street out there, those are the limits of his domain. That's how it works."

Her voice had softened and another soul was staring at me from behind Rita's dark, dark eyes. Suddenly I couldn't breathe. I wanted to scream, to howl.

"Kate?"

"She's a passenger," Rita was back, all husky voice and sex-in-a-smile. "It's an expensive ride but apparently you're worth it."

"I don't understand... Kate..."

"Breast cancer, spread to the lymph nodes. She always wanted to come back to you, kept putting it off then suddenly it was too late, although it's never too late if you're prepared to pay. She wants to save you, and I can see why." Her hand went to my face.

I flinched back. "What are you?"

"Let's just say that Possession can go both ways. The difference is that this way round it's voluntary and we don't send for the priest, we just charge a fare."

I stared at her, into her eyes, desperate to see Kate again, but there was only darkness. "Where is Arnold Cryer?" I hissed, angry, distraught.

"Where you sent him, Martin."

7: Brawl

The piano burst into life, the sound as jangly and battered as the instrument it came from. The musician was a large woman with garish lipstick and a dress that was too small for her considerable bulk. She had a cigarette clamped firmly in the corner of her mouth. A few people gathered round and someone started to sing *Roll out the Barrel*. Others joined in.

I felt Rita, or was it Kate, squeeze my hand briefly. She got to her feet and brushed past me, close enough to murmur "I think this is what you'd call a Jam Nite," in my ear then nodded towards a door at the end of the bar. Her breath was hot and moist. She moved away from me. The singalong had ended and the punters were clapping and whistling.

The crowd parted so that Rita could get to the piano. "I'd like to sing for you now," she said and the crowd cheered enthusiastically.

"What's your name, love?" said the pianist.

"Rita," she answered, but the voice was Kate's. Then Rita again. "I'm going to bring some class to the occasion."

"What'll it be?" the pianist asked.

"Thank you, but I won't need an accompaniment."

There were amiably sarcastic ohhs and aaahs, and a shout of "Bit of a prima donna this one."

She began to sing and I almost broke. Kate's voice was clear and achingly beautiful and filled the pub with light and, of course, the song was *Un bel dì vedremo*. The punters were transfixed. Tears streamed down many of their faces, and down Rita's, cutting molten trails through her mascara and rouge.

I wrenched myself free of her spell and rushed the door. I almost made it unnoticed. Almost.

My hand was on the doorknob...

"Oi!"

A roar drowned Kate's voice and the crowd rose up as one and surged towards me, suddenly grotesque in the wan orange light with their bad teeth and shabby clothes. The nearest was a fleshy mountain of a man whose face was round to the point of being spherical and whose eyes were tiny black pinpricks. He opened his mouth and I saw that bad dentistry had turned to needle fangs.

Behind him, the pianist had finally burst free of her too-small dress to reveal a body covered with bestial raging heads, each one affixed to her flesh via a thin, snake-like neck, snarling and hissing, mouths lined with sharp teeth.

I spun round and snatched up a chair just as fatman threw himself into the attack. I swung the chair hard, felt wood crunch against flesh. The creature staggered to one side.

The pianist was on me next. I thrust the chair at her, legs first, jabbed and danced. A thin character in a military-surplus greatcoat with the head of a bird darted in. The chair arced round; birdman was down, but the pianist was through the gap.

I stumbled against the door, saw the heads, the venom-dripping fangs.

Then something huge and raging swept down on her to rip her torso apart and spill a million shiny, black, scrabbling cockroaches onto the dark-stained, wooden floor. Rita, taloned and snake-tongued, slashed and gouged flesh in a demonic, berserker fury of unthinkable violence.

She screamed "Run!" and it was Kate.

I slammed open the door and all-but fell down a narrow, slippery stone stairway.

8: Caterpillar

There was light, poor, dirty and with no visible source. The stairs ended at the entrance to a narrow passageway, roofed by an arch of mouldy-looking, cobweb-infested bricks.

As I ran, half-crouched, I glimpsed scuttling things and slithering things. I felt moistures drip into my hair. Heard...

Breathing, growing louder than the rapidly fading battle noise. The breathing was laboured and emphysema-ridden. My name was repeated over and over and melded into the lung-sick rattle.

I slowed. I could not see that old bastard again.

Marty boy, please... You owe me son.

"I'm not your son," I whispered, breathless myself now.

I never hurt you, did I, never raised a hand to you.

The brawl grew louder. I broke into a run, lurched round bends and bumped against the foul, dank wall. And finally stumbled into a low-roofed chamber, just managing to come to a halt before careering into...

It.

Him.

Something.

The thing was huge and horrible to the point of obscene. The thing was a worm, a huge, many-segmented vastness. There was no head that I could see.

It lay on the foul, stone floor, expanding and contracting with every laboured breath. Inhalation was announced by long, shuddering groans, exhalation marked by puffs of noxious fumes from holes in its skin. Things crawled over its hide, rat-sized but many-legged, too fast for me to comprehend their geometries.

Help me Martin, please...please help me boy.

I did this.

Thirteen I was. Man enough to be culpable. Man enough to know exactly what I was doing when I told my school teacher that my stepfather had touched me.

"I lied," I said. "I lied... I'm sorry."

You didn't have to do that.

"You stole my mum." My voice was a child's voice now. "You took her away from me and my dad."

It takes two to tango, boy. She didn't take much stealing and your old chap didn't take much pushing. He'd already found his comfort the arms of another. He'd been seeing her for years.

The sound of the brawl edged into the chamber, roars and squeals, snarls and gibbering.

The caterpillar thing coughed, a long messy fit of brutal hacking.

There had been rows, I remembered that now, clashes, muted by the bedroom floor. Mum screeching, dad's faltering calm, boiling towards apocalypse then sudden silence. But that was marriage, wasn't it? A relentless riff of devotion, irritation, hurt then release. Hadn't Kate screamed at me as often as she had loved me, sobbed and pummelled me with her tiny knotted fists then collapsed into my arms as I stood, helpless and pathetic and drunk or stoned or both? Useless to her and yet hers and hers alone.

Why, then, couldn't I remember similar clashes between Arnold Cryer, that feral charmer and mother-thief, and the object of his crime? Why do I recall that the only bitter fire-fights of that period were between mum and me, with the imposter trying to act as conciliator before retreating under the venom of my adolescent loathing?

I was dying anyway Marty. It was the best way, get it over with.

He was doing it again, trying too hard, twisting the truth to... to what? To protect the stepson he had adopted, in his shambolic, clumsy way.

Cryer had hanged himself because of me. A lonely, broken-down, diseased wreck of a man, the Scrubs quickly exchanged for a grey-walled, psychiatric concentration camp.

And still mum had stood by him...

I only want you to do one thing boy.

I couldn't...

Please lad, come on, it can't hurt can it?

I shook my head, snuffled messily and realised that I was crying. Me, the big, ugly harp player from an almost-famous, notoriously booze-sodden blues band, sobbing and shaking my head and unable to save the man I had condemned.

Rita stumbled into the chamber. Her hat was gone, coat ripped, her dress torn and bloody. She folded, head down, hands on her knees. Her hair fell about her sweat-slicked face.

"I held them off... off for as long ...long as I could... You have to hurry."

Then she looked up at me and seemed to see me for the first time. She stumbled forwards and grabbed my arms.

"Martin, please, you have to do it," Kate said.

I couldn't speak.

Shadows reached into the chamber, shadows and babel.

I swung round and lurched towards the pulsing, trembling caterpillar-thing.

I moved close and froze.

Please lad, come on, it can't hurt can it?

How many times had he said that to me? Him standing there, arm about my mum's shoulders, her head leaning against him, smiling that bloody smile he had given her. Him with his hand extended in friendship. How many times had he offered me that hand, just a measly bloody handshake, that one, tiny point of acceptable male contact?

Rita went down as the horde exploded into the chamber. I cried out for Kate, my voice lost in the cacophony.

Then reached out and touched the flesh of the creature I had hated from the moment I first saw him.

There was no sensation.

Nothing.

But a flicker of light and shadow, like the flutter of wings.

9: Fare

Fog.

A Blitz-wounded street.

And an elegant, dark-haired woman, her fur coat open to reveal a blue dress with a Bardot-neckline, her face hidden by the shadow of a broad-brimmed hat.

I swallowed. "That fare, you know, the one Kate is supposed to pay, can't you…"

"Can the universe stop expanding? Can energy disappear?"

"Please don't hurt her… her soul…"

I felt Rita's stare though I couldn't see her eyes. "Do you remember the song?" she said. "Kate's performance?"

I nodded.

"Do you remember my face?"

I had seen Kate's tears.

"*Were* they Kate's?" She paused. "Don't fear for her. All I ask in payment is for her to sing to me when the rigours of eternity become too tiresome to endure, David's harp to Saul's rage."

That's all I wanted too.

"You know how to get home."

She came to me and slid her arms about me and I smelled Kate's perfume, tasted Kate on her lips and swallowed tears. I wasn't sure whose they were.

Then she was gone and there was only the smog-choked street. I drew the harmonica from my jacket pocket.

Long Train Runnin'

1

There was a trainset displayed in the warm-lit window of the Age Concern shop; two carriages, a set of tracks, a station, a tunnel and a sleek, green Britannia class steam locomotive, all fitted snugly into their mouldings in a large, rectangular cardboard box. The box's yellow flashings and *Triang-Hornby* logos stirred something in Ray Whitley's soul he knew he should have outgrown forty-odd years ago.

Christmas Eve rain lashed at him as he stared through the grubby glass and wondered why he felt a need to go inside and buy the lot. For Nathan of course. Not that his grandson needed another present. The boy would be drowning in them tomorrow, and Ray had already bought him a new bicycle.

The charity shop itself would be closing in a few minutes. He experienced a frisson of panic brought on by indecision...

The door bleeped as he stepped inside.

"How much?" he asked the assistant. She was a teenager, bright-eyed and full of smiles.

"Ten pounds," she said.

"*How* much?"

"Is that too expensive? I could phone the manager—"

"No, what I mean is, stuff like this is worth a fortune."

"Is it?"

"Look, I'll give you thirty quid, and I'm still robbing you blind."

He's not going to want this, Ray told himself as walked away from the shop. He's a twenty-first century boy; his entertainment is digital, virtual. What the hell is he going to make of a fifty year old train-set?

Fifty years.

The toy in the *Age Concern* carrier bag was older than Nathan would ever be.

2

There were no decorations in Ray's flat. No point. There *were* photographs however; his son Dave, child, adult, husband now father; Nathan, of course, from baby to six. And Chrissie, Ray's wife of thirty-years.

They had married back in 1980, she 19 and gorgeous, he 25, handsome but nervous and showing it through his daft grin. Chrissie had progressed from pretty to elegant; Ray, from good-looking rascal to sleek rascal. Or so he liked to believe.

Ray sold carpets in one of the big out-of-town stores. He used to enjoy it. Difficult to enjoy much at all these days, since Chrissie had driven her car through a red light into the path of a truck.

Four years ago.

It was his fault. Chrissie was a careful driver, but the trauma of discovering your husband had had an affair was not conducive to road safety.

Ray sipped whisky. He was aware that he sipped too much whisky, just as he smoked too many cigarettes.

But what else was there?

Well, there was Nathan.

Ray choked back a sob, the kind that would suddenly burst out of him lately.

Enough, he admonished himself, *this Christmas belongs to the boy.* Everyone had agreed to make it as normal as possible, even down to granddad being allowed to spend the day at his son's house for the first time since Chrissie's death.

Forgiveness was a slow process. But it *was* underway. It had started with outings – father, son and family meeting up on neutral ground, to allow Nathan to bond with his granddad, for them all to find a way through the darkness.

Even so, tomorrow was going to be bloody difficult.

3

Nervously, Ray unloaded the gleaming new bicycle from the boot of his car then dragged the train set from the passenger seat. He carried the parcel and the bike towards his son's house, an anonymous semi in an anonymous cul-de-sac.

In coldly pragmatic terms, the bike was a waste of money, but Nathan was desperate for a new bicycle so Ray had been happy to oblige. He might get a lot more use out of it than anyone anticipated.

His daughter-in-law's parents were already here, Ray had noticed their 4x4 parked directly outside the house. The prospect of a day with Tony and Michelle Anderson did not fill him with delight.

A moment, then the door opened and Nathan was beaming up at him, eyes bright.

"Granddad!" he shouted and clutched Ray's legs tightly.

Ray ruffled non-existent hair on the boy's chemo-bald scalp.

"What have you got, granddad? Is it a bike, is it a bike?"

"Oh yeah, *my* bike. I cycled here, I need the exercise."

"It's too small. You'd squash it. Is that my bike? Is it?"

"What do you think?"

"It is!"

"Come on, Nathe," Dave said. "Let the poor old man in, it's freezing out there."

Ray struggled the bike into the hallway, Nathan under his feet, almost beside himself with joy.

"Thanks dad," Dave sounded tense, but his brief man-hug seemed genuine.

Okay, time to go into the lounge.

The sheer number and extravagance of the presents strewn around the Christmas tree was shocking. Nathan ran round in circles. He picked things up and put them down. He crouched, crawled, *swam* in presents. A frail little snow-pale boy, given a spell of remission by the god who had decreed that not only was the family to lose one of its women to a car crash, it must also lose one of its newest members to leukaemia.

Dave's wife was Jemma. She was a capable young woman with dark hair and startling blue eyes. Dave worked as a carpenter, Jemma worked in a bank. Today she looked as tired and pale as her son. She talked too quickly and laughed too readily and when she gave Ray a hug, he could feel her trembling.

"How're you doing Ray?" Jemma's father called from the sofa. He was a tanned, silver fox.

"Not so bad, you?"

"Pretty good."

"Michelle," Ray said and offered his hand to Jemma's mother. Her smile was brief and tight. Michelle Anderson was even more tanned than her husband, her short hair dyed a harsh blonde, her earrings ludicrously huge.

"You look well," Ray said.

"Couple of weeks in the time-share; Michelle needed a break," Tony answered. "She spends a lot of time here with Jemma and... you know."

Was it now forbidden to speak Nathan's name?

He remembered the parcel under his arm and was suddenly embarrassed.

"I bought Nathan something else," he said.

"I think there's another inch of space over there," Dave joked and everyone produced a laugh.

He handed the present to Nathan, who set about ripping it open with brutal efficiency. For a moment he stared at the box, and frowned as if he didn't know what it was. An embarrassed silence fell.

"A train," Nathan said at last. "Like *Thomas the Tank Engine?*"

"Yeah, but for grown-ups," Ray said.

Nathan gazed at the locomotive and carriages with something resembling awe.

4

A fumbling of track and wires then on with the power. The controller comprised a metal box, an on-off switch and a big red dial which controlled the locomotive's speed and direction.

"Okay Nathan, all you have to do is turn the dial. That's it, nice and smooth."

Nathan's concentration was fierce. Outside, the cloud-dulled Christmas afternoon was already turning dark. Rain hammered at the window.

There was, Ray knew, some resentment at his taking Nathan up here to play with the train set. Everyone wanted *a piece of the boy* – an overused Hollywood cliché but so true.

Ray chuckled. "It goes backwards as well."

Nathan wasn't listening. He was transfixed. His fingers worked the controller with the delicacy of a veteran.

5

There had been light, in the carriages.

Ray wrestled with the memory as he stood on his flat's balcony and smoked a pre-bed cigarette.

There were, of course, *no* lights in those carriages. He couldn't even remember the moment he saw them – or *thought* he saw them.

There were no bloody lights.

~

"I'm afraid Nathan is suffering from acute myeloid leukaemia," said the shockingly young oncologist.

Chrissie was there that day, holding Jemma's hand because Jemma's own parents were flying home from yet another Costa del Sol time-share break. "It's caused by an overproduction of immature white myeloid cells, which prevent the bone marrow from making healthy blood cells. There's an increased risk of infection." He paused, uncomfortable. "AML is very rare."

"What will happen to him?" Dave sounded frighteningly calm. "How long…"

The doctor swallowed. "Children with AML do not have a positive outlook. However…" He held up his hands, as if to still a rising (though non-existent) storm of panic from his audience. "If caught early, as in Nathan's case, the prognosis improves significantly."

"Thank God," Chrissie breathed and grabbed Ray's hand with her free one. Her skin was hot and damp.

That was when Ray realised that the two-year old Nathan was no longer in the doctor's office.

Ray tried to tell the others, but no one was listening. He got up, made for the door, his movements slow, awkward. He fumbled at the door handle, pulled the door open and stepped out into…

Fog, so dense he could barely see anything. He coughed; the mist was warm, and had an oily flavour. Not fog at all. Steam.

A small figure, up ahead, seen, then gone.

"Nathan, come back."

The steam cleared a little and the monster was revealed; a vast locomotive. It hissed, snarled and snorted steam. Its wheels were vast. Its complexity of pistons gleamed with oiled perfection. The thing was all trapped fury and chained power. The thing was terrifying.

The thing was hungry.

Ray saw Nathan, not two anymore, but six. Ray tried to run, but his legs were all but unusable. The steam cleared again. A carriage door had opened. Light spilled out, hot orange light, flickering like the flame-glow from the train's firebox.

Nathan was framed in the door, silhouetted against the hell-light, one foot on the platform, the other in the carriage. Ray screamed the boy's name but his voice was shredded by the deafening blast of a train whistle—

He sat up in bed, gasping for air, his mouth fouled with hot, oil-flavoured steam. The train whistle rang on through the dark and faded into the distant hum of night-traffic and a far-off police siren.

6

"Oh hello," Jemma said when she opened the door to Ray the next day. "I thought you'd be at work."

Boxing Day. Ray had phoned in sick, the first time he had ever lied to his boss. "Just thought I'd see how things are."

And check if there really are any lights in the train set...

Jemma managed a smile. "Come in. Mum and Dad are here."

Ray knew that already, he had seen the 4x4.

"Ray!" Tony offered one of his best-mates-but-not-really handshakes.

Dave came into the lounge. "Hello dad," he said. "Cuppa? We've just put the kettle on."

"Please." He needed more than caffeine at that moment. "Where's Nathan, is he all right?"

Dave smiled ruefully. "He's upstairs, playing with that train set you bought him."

Michelle made a *tsk* sound. "It's not good for him to be stuck in his room."

The tea arrived and Ray forced himself to drink it before asking if he could go up and see his grandson.

Tony and Michelle exchanged looks of disapproval. But it was Jemma who laughed and said; "He'll be really pleased to see you. He's driven us crazy all morning talking about trains and signals and god knows what else."

There were no lights, no steam, no clanking iron fury. Just a little boy and an ancient plastic train. Ray knelt down and ruffled his grandson's imaginary hair.

"How're you doing?" he said.

"Mmmm," Nathan said.

The locomotive drove into the tunnel entrance.

"Nathan," Ray said quietly.

No response. For a moment Ray wondered if the train's endless oval circling had hypnotised the boy.

"Nathan," he said again and this time reached out to gently shake his grandson's bony shoulder.

Nathan uttered a small gasp of shock and looked round sharply. He blinked as if trying to remember where he was, then smiled and threw his skinny arms round Ray's neck. "Granddad!"

7

"We're going out for lunch I'm afraid," Michelle said when Ray went back downstairs.

"That's okay," Ray answered. "I've got a few things to do–"

"Come with us," Dave said. "It's just a pub lunch."

"It *is* Boxing Day, remember," Tony said. "We had to book-up in advance to get this table."

"Oh, I'm sure they'll find another seat for us," Jemma answered. She set off to fetch Nathan.

"Thanks, I'd love to come." Ray was enjoying Tony and Michelle's annoyance.

There was a commotion from upstairs; Jemma, angry, Nathan wailing in enraged protest. Michelle was on her feet in a moment. Tony put his hand on her arm. "Don't interfere," he said, but she ignored him and bounded up the stairs to do just that.

~

"It's your fault," Dave joked as they took their seats in the pub. "He didn't want to leave that bloody train set."

"Kids eh?" Tony said, "He'll soon get tired of it."

And then he can numb his brain by killing aliens on that Wii you bought him, Ray added silently. The pub was packed, hot and noisy. The food, when it came, was bland and the helpings impoverished. Still it was food and Ray was hungry. He hadn't eaten since yesterday.

The walk home took them past the cemetery. Its grand entrance was made bleak by the iron-grey sky and leafless trees that overarched its wrought-iron splendour. Glimpsed beyond the gates' black bars was a desolate landscape of grey headstones and winter-bleached grass.

You'll be lonely in there Nathan...

Ray grabbed his grandson's hand. The boy seemed unaware and continued chattering away with no need for punctuation.

"...more tracks," he said. "And I like that engine because it's green and fast and looks really cool and there's people in the carriages..."

People?

"What people, Nathan?" Ray kept his voice matter-of-fact. "What people did you see in the carriages?"

Nathan chuckled. "There aren't any people in the carriages, they're too small, people aren't that small."

~

"Smoke?" Dave said when they arrived back at the house.

The two of them wandered out to the garden shed.

"You ought to give those things a miss," Ray told his son as they lit up.

"It's bloody hard dad." Dave's voice was suddenly near to breaking. "I can't... you know, imagine it really happening."

"Perhaps it won't." Ray was immediately angry with himself for offering such a useless platitude. This was a precious moment, a fragile component drawn from the jackstraw structure of their reconciliation.

"Sometimes I wish it would just happen, that we could get it over with." Dave slumped back against the shed's damp wooden wall, pain torn into his face. "Is that wrong?"

"No, it's not wrong."

Dave looked away across the small, neat garden. Night was falling. "What'll it be like for Nathan... what it'll feel like to die and be in the dark? He's scared of the dark dad..." His voice broke and Ray reached out to grasp his son's right shoulder.

"Perhaps it isn't dark," Ray said.

Perhaps it's the colour of twisting, flickering, hot, hot flame...

He glanced up. Nathan's bedroom light was on. The boy was in his room, playing with the train set no doubt. Good.

Because it was only a train set and there were neither lights, people nor fire in those little plastic carriages.

Indoors Tony and Michelle were drinking coffee and watching

television.

"Jemma's putting Nathan to bed," Tony explained. "She had a bit of a fight with him while you two were puffing away out there." Sarcastic disapproval disguised as a joke, Tony's speciality.

"It's that train set," Michelle added.

Before Ray could reply Jemma came downstairs.

"He wants granddad to read him a story," she said.

Both Ray and Tony made to get up.

"Granddad Whitley." She gave an apologetic shrug to her dad, who didn't seem too bothered. Her mother, however, looked ready to commit murder.

8

Ray stepped carefully over the train set to sit on Nathan's bed. The boy had chosen a battered *Thomas the Tank Engine* omnibus as his story book.

Nathan burrowed under the duvet while Ray read, enjoying himself so much he carried on reading even after Nathan was asleep. The dim, orange bedside lamp carved deep shadows into the boy's face. He looked peaceful—

The little locomotive suddenly burst into life and raced along the track, dragging its carriages behind.

Unable to speak, unable to comprehend, Ray stared down at the hurtling train. Light spilled from the carriages, flame and smoke poured from the minute chimney, the whistle shrieked.

He dropped to his knees, grabbed the controller and tried to turn the thing off. The train accelerated, faster and faster. Ray saw the people then, through the tiny windows of the carriages, faces, staring out, mouths wide open.

Screaming.

Nathan was awake, instantly, no bleary transition. He scrambled from the bed, dropped to his knees, stared, laughed and reached out towards the train.

Ray scrabbled at the wires, wrenched them free. No effect. Round and round it went, flame-light glinting in its carriage windows, tiny souls howling for mercy. Ray grabbed at the engine, but snatched back his hand. He couldn't touch it. It was like a rat, a slithering, vicious thing.

So he surged across the track and took hold of Nathan instead. The boy's delight turned to anguish. He howled, struggled and drove his fist into Ray's mouth, breaking skin. Ray shouted, out of control, wild with fear. He had to get the screeching, writhing boy out of this room, away from the train.

9

Despite the Winter Sales, business was slow. Ray paced the shop, head pounding, tired from lack of sleep. It was New Year's Eve. The carpet store was open until six; another hour and three-quarters before he could go home.

And then what?

He had been back to his son's house twice since *the incident*. Both times he had been sent away. Nathan was too upset and frightened to see him. There had been no calls, no contact for three days now. He knew he should ring Dave but he couldn't bring himself to pick up the phone. Instead he sat at home, smoking and drinking and wallowing in his misery before crawling into bed or falling asleep on the sofa and plunging straight into the nightmare.

The same one, every night; the train with its flame-lit windows and those faces, begging for release, old and young, men, women and children, desperate, stolen.

Damned.

And then he would see Nathan, a vague figure in the mist, making for the open carriage door and he would call the boy's name and try to reach him, but was always too late.

Ray headed back through the maze of carpet rolls towards his desk.

God, he had fought hard to regain what he had lost. And now he had torn apart the fragile threads of filial reconciliation with that moment of insanity on Boxing Day evening.

Ray rubbed his face with clammy, trembling hands. He needed to go to bed.

A train whistle blew, shrill, harsh, ripping into his skull.

It became the stabbing trill of his iPhone.

"Dad," Dave's voice was horribly controlled. "Nathan's in hospital."

10

Nathan was in a side-room, a pale smear of near-translucent flesh on the pillow. There were tubes and a drip. His breathing was shallow and irregular. Dave sat on the bed, Tony and Michelle on hard chairs. Jemma, in the obligatory hospital armchair, was totally absorbed with her son. She clutched his tiny, white hand and murmured softly.

Dave caught Ray's eye. He shook his head, the movement so slight it was barely perceptible.

"I'll see if I can find a chair," Ray said at last. "Does anyone want a tea or coffee?"

No one did.

Back in the main ward area Ray slumped against the wall and caught his breath. Christ he needed a cigarette. Something snagged his attention. He glanced round and saw a child, walking towards the doors, heading out of the ward.

Careless. Where the hell were the kid's parents?

It was a young boy, wearing a hospital gown. His skin was pale, his scalp denuded by chemotherapy...

Ray's breath caught in his throat.

"Nathan!"

But he was gone.

11

Wondering if he had gone insane, Ray reversed his car erratically out of his parking space and made for the exit. He realised that his family would probably never talk to him again for this desertion in their time of need, but Ray had seen his grandson leave that ward, had seen his shade, his soul, his spirit, and knew where he was going.

The snowfall grew heavier while the radio murmured excitedly about blocked roads and accidents. Ray was sweating, he felt sick, his left arm ached.

Light, straight ahead, a searing white glare that hid something huge, fast and pummelling straight towards him. Ray saw fire, belching from a chimney stack, steam and spark. A train, it was a bloody train...

He hit the brakes; the car slewed left. A violent impact juddered through him. Something shattered, metal crunched. Light flooded the car, the roar of steam and iron wheels, power and weight exploded out of the snow-mad night—

A bus.

Ray shouldered the door open and walked away. He saw that his car was rammed into the side of a parked saloon. That could wait. They'd find him, licence number, Swansea and the rest.

His mobile phone was ringing. He fumbled it from his pocket and saw that it was Dave.

He couldn't stop now.

12

Dave and Jemma's house was dark. Ray had no key.

He peered round the cul-de-sac, eyes screwed up against the sting of the wind-blown snow. There, a pile of bricks, someone rebuilding a garden wall. He grabbed three of them.

The first ricocheted off the lounge window. The second cracked the glass. The third shattered the window.

Ray clambered into the gap and felt glass tear at his hands and his clothes. Pain and blood didn't matter. Not now. He fell into the lounge, ending up on top of the coffee table, which collapsed under him.

The house shook suddenly with the roar of the train, the pounding of its iron wheels, the thud of its pistons. Steam misted the air. Ray coughed and gagged on the hot oily stench. Pain began to spread from his left arm and across his chest.

Ray could see the door to Nathan's bedroom. Light spilled from under it, uncertain flickering. Ray forced himself up the last remaining steps and onto the landing. He grabbed at Nathan's door; it gave way and he dropped to his knees on the threshold.

And there it was, hurtling round and bloody round. Light blazed from its carriage windows and cast lunatic shadows on the wall above the bed.

Nathan, still in his hospital gown, was on the bed, reaching toward the shadow carriage with his small, ghost-white hand. Ray launched himself at the train. A wave of pain ripped through his chest and stole his breath. He came to rest lying across the track. The train raced away from him. He craned his neck and saw Nathan, all but camouflaged by the wild shadow-carriage. All but devoured...

Ray watched the train turn the corner then head for the tunnel opposite where he lay. If he could just reach out and grab the engine... but he couldn't move, he could *not* touch that foul thing.

Had to...

The locomotive was cold. It burned his flesh and sent shockwaves into his already staggering heart. His head was filled with its roar as it writhed in his hand, vile and alive.

He smashed it down onto the floor.

Again, again, again...

Suddenly it was dark and still. His iPhone warbled. He didn't answer. He knew.

Because of the gentle passage of something free and love-filled that brushed his cheek like a child's kiss, and was gone.

INCUBUS

1

"You're quiet." There was no concern in Daniel's voice, but neither was there anger. There was never anger. His words always seemed carefully-chosen, his tone pitch-perfect.

"Just thinking," Kristen said.

"You weren't quiet at the party. You were talking, to everyone."

"It was good to see our friends." *Our* friends? They were her friends. Kristen had never met Daniel's friends. "I was having fun."

"I could see that."

Kristen had been through this before and it wasn't what she wanted tonight. She pulled her fur coat tightly about herself, and not because Daniel's car was cold.

"I'm sorry." She was always sorry. She couldn't seem to get this right. Perhaps, and it wasn't the first time she had allowed this thought in from the outer darkness, it was because she wasn't good at relationships. Perhaps she had never fully grasped the mechanics of intimacy.

She had certainly got it wrong last time, and had the decree nisi to prove it.

She stole a glance at Daniel, a patchwork of silhouette and glimpsed features, lit intermittently by the brief flares of oncoming headlights and the orange flicker of street lamps. Daniel with his dramatic, swept-back hair, broad shoulders and a face any self-respecting writer of romance would describe as *chiselled*. A catch worth fighting for.

Catch? God, she was becoming her own mother.

Kristen sought a topic of conversation, something to break the silence. "I thought Paul didn't look too well." It sounded lame in her ears, the words thick and clumsy in her mouth.

"Can't say I noticed."

"He's under a lot of stress."

"You asked him, did you?"

"Well, yes."

"I'm sure he appreciated your concern."

"Are you jealous? I mean, he's a good friend of mine, that's all..."

"I'm jealous because you had a proper conversation with him."

"Oh come on, Daniel. You can't expect me to cling to you like a limpet every time we go to a party."

"Of course not, but there's the sublime, Kristen, and there's the ridiculous."

Dulled, Kristen reached for the car radio and found some late night ballads. They didn't help. The singers all seemed to understand the complexities of relationships far better than she did, even when those relationships were soured.

There must be something she could talk about, something that would slice through the suffocating blank that seemed to have settled over her brain.

They arrived home at the flat she shared with Daniel, *her* flat.

Despite wanting nothing more than to shed them like old skin, Kristen kept her fur coat, dress and heels in place. She had to make amends. She had to break the dark mood that had smothered the evening.

Daniel kicked off his shoes, slumped onto the sofa and reached for the music centre remote. "Can't sleep," he mumbled. Bebop twittered from the expensive speakers he had installed in the lounge; Charlie Parker's *Ornithology*. Kristen had learned a lot about jazz from Daniel.

Kristen sat beside him, self-conscious in her clothes, feeling suddenly clumsy in the art of allure and seduction. She moved close. No response. She nuzzled and kissed his neck.

"I'm too agitated," he said and shrugged himself away from her. "Get to bed, I'll be up later." There was no cruelty in voice, He was never cruel.

As she lay in the dark, Kristen tried to work out when, and how, this whole thing had soured.

Had it soured?

They had been together (an item, wasn't that what it was called?) for four months now. Kristen had been out with friends, led by Sarah, on a campaign to drag her back into the wide world after the divorce. Daniel had been in one of the nightclubs they had visited, unmissable, an intriguing, striking figure at the bar. His hair, face, his presence, were somehow over-perfect, theatrical almost, yet unaffected. He glanced her way and she was smitten; archaic word, but what other word was there? Kristen tried to ignore him. She didn't like being made so ridiculous by her own rekindled lust.

She wanted to leave the club.

She wanted him to ask her for a dance.

They didn't leave the club and suddenly Daniel was standing over her, smiling and holding out his hand. He didn't ask. He didn't have to.

He moved into her flat six weeks later. The usual new-love delirium survived for a few more weeks after that. Then, imperceptibly, insidiously, the dynamic shifted. Or was it merely an admission of how things had been from the start? She the rabbit frozen in the headlights, he the oncoming car.

Her health had suffered as well. Coincidence of course, and nothing she could put her finger on. Bouts of mild flu-symptoms, an undertow of weariness, ailments that did not prevent her from functioning and could be explained away by periods, work-stress, the bumps and bruises of modern living.

But none of these things mattered, when, in the quiet dark, he touched her...

Self-pity seeped through the fissures in Kristen's hurt. She wondered, again, if she was good enough for him. A pathetic idea, she knew. And even if it was true, surely it was down to her to make herself *good enough* for him.

No, the other Kristen snapped, the hard-arsed, tough-as-nails version of Kristen that inhabited her head, but seldom her skin anymore. *It's his fault. He's the bastard. He's abusive, passive-aggressive, the worst kind, the deceiver, the blamer, the manipulator. It's your flat, your life, your soul. You should get rid of him, tell him to leave.*

And cast herself back into the cold, wasteland of the world. Is that what she wanted? To lose her *catch*?

The thought followed her down into the dark.

Where she became aware of pleasure, waves of it that drew her back towards consciousness, opened by small kisses, and his sure, familiar touch. Her mouth dried, her breathing became ragged. She rolled onto her back and slid her arms about him and tasted his flesh on her lips. Then he filled her and the pleasures of it forced gasps, then cries, out of her.

Afterwards she curled herself into his arms and lived the moment in his warmth.

"I love you," she whispered. "I'm sorry..."

2

The bed was empty when Kristen woke. Her head ached. A minor hangover, she supposed, although she had not drunk a great deal last night.

Ah, last night. She smiled, winced. Paracetamol needed. She swung her legs out of the bed, waiting for an unexpected wash of dizziness to pass, before she headed into the kitchen, where she found Daniel brewing coffee and buttering toast. He smiled.

"What shall we do today?" he asked.

"A walk," Kristen said. She needed to clear her head.

"Where?"

She panicked. Ridiculous, but she could never think where to walk, though it was not for want of places; there were towpaths, footpaths, parks and country inns aplenty within easy reach.

"Sarratt." Automatic answer. Their favourite place.

"Tired of it. We go there too often."

"Hampstead Heath? We could have lunch at the Saracen's Head."

"Don't feel like going into town." He frowned, a sign of deep thought. "I know; the Downs, Ivinghoe Beacon."

And if you had suggested Ivinghoe? Hard-Arsed Kristen said. *He would have rejected the idea; too far away, too cold, too bleak. You can't win this game, girl.*

Let him win. Did it really fucking matter?

God she was tired. Again.

Christ, she wasn't pregnant was she? Impossible. She was careful.

But if she was, would it matter?

The thought stayed with her as she made her way into the flat's small lounge. She slumped onto the sofa, in need of a rest. The flat was cramped. It had been okay when she bought it, because it had been just for her. Then it had seemed like paradise, a refuge from a very broken marriage. Her own place.

Kristen's phone rang.

It was Sarah. "You free, Krissy?"

"Uh... I don't know... I..."

"A coffee? That's all. I need some coffee and friendship." A pause. "Hussein's left me."

"When?"

"Friday. It was why I wasn't at that bloody party last night." A sardonic chuckle. "I've stopped crying now, and moved on to the need-coffee-with-my-best-mate stage."

"Hang on... I'll ask Daniel..."

Who had just stepped into the lounge, breakfast tray in hand.

"I need to meet up with Sarah."

"Why?"

"She needs to talk to me about something."

"Now? On a Sunday morning?"

Kristen shrugged, and felt herself make an I-know-this-is-a-pain-but-she-needs-me face. She was immediately guilty, and angered by her own dishonesty.

Tell him, for God's sake. Don't ask, tell *the bastard you're going out.*

"How long are you going to be?"

"Cup of coffee." Since when had that been a unit of time?

"Just make sure you're back for us to go out to lunch."

Kristen tried not to admit to pathetic gratitude as she dressed, pulled on her coat and grabbed the keys to her own car. But self-honesty assured her that this was exactly what it was.

"You look terrible."

Kristen was taken aback. "I'm sorry?"

"You're as white as a sheet, Krissy."

"The party...you know..."

"Doesn't look like a hangover to me."

They were in Costa. Kristen had just arrived, standing by the table, coat on. Sarah looked a little delicate herself, but she was tough and that part of her was already winning through. She was immaculate; new cream blouse, her hair shimmering, exuberantly blonde.

"You're exhausted," Sarah said, as if pressing home the attack.

"Working too hard..."

Sarah looked sceptical. "No it's not. God, are you..."

"No" A little too loud and defensive. "I'm not pregnant."

"Are you and Daniel okay?"

"We're fine, why do you think—"

"You know I don't like him, Krissy. He's not right for you."

"You've told me before, a lot of times, but he *feels* right to me." Kristen had finally taken off her coat and sat down. "Anyway, I'm here for *you* Sarah."

"I know. I'm sorry." Sarah sipped coffee, stared out of the window for few moments before continuing. "Now I've had time to sulk, I'm fine, I think. Hussein was a good guy, but it wouldn't have lasted. He was too nice, I suppose, nice bordering on boring. To be fair, I gave the poor bastard a hard time. Nothing he did was right. He's better off without me."

"So, he just upped and left?"

"Yep. Said that's it, grabbed his stuff and walked out. I didn't exactly go down on my knees and beg him to stay."

Outside it had begun to rain. The North London street, already winter dull, was finally turned to grey mush.

"You should do the same, Krissy."

"What?"

"Tell Daniel to pack up *his* stuff and leave."

"Please stop this..."

"He's sucking the life out of you."

"I think you need to stop—"

"You had to ask his permission to come and see me, Krissy. I heard you over the phone. You don't need to ask anyone's permission to see a friend. He doesn't own you."

Kristen was on her feet, grabbing her coat, fumbling with her purse. "It's none of your business, Sarah. I came here to help you. I didn't come here for you to insult the person I love and accuse me of..." Of what?

Clenched into panic, Kristen hurried through the packed confines of the café, to the door which wouldn't open because it was supposed to be pulled, not pushed. She could hear Sarah calling to her, apologising. Then she was outside.

Kristen reached her car, fumbled the keys and managed to bundle herself into the driver's seat. Rain drummed the roof, blurred the view through the windscreen. She needed to calm down, she needed to breathe.

She didn't want to go home.

But where else was there to go?

3

For the first time since she had joined this company as a project manager, Kristen was too distracted to work. Worse still, there was a progress meeting after lunch. The prospect was a dull one.

The reason for her malaise was no mystery.

Daniel had punished her.

Even though she returned home early from her coffee with Sarah. Even though she devoted the rest of her Sunday to him. He had punished her.

Hadn't he?

Did he beat her? No. Did he rage and scream and crumple her self-belief with vicious words? No. He was affable, polite. They walked, on Hampstead Heath, because they could think of nowhere else. It was too late for Ivinghoe and any suggestions Kristen came up with were quietly but firmly rejected. So they walked where he hadn't wanted to walk and in his mysterious way, he made sure that Kristen was ill-at-ease because of yet another failure.

They ate at the Saracen's Head. Once the rain cleared, the day was winter bright. Daniel held her hand. He chatted, a little, and Kristen worked hard at keeping the conversation flowing.

In the evening they sat together on the sofa and watched their favourite Sunday night television; a political thriller, a half-hour satirical panel game. Then they went to bed. Where they made... love? They touched, expertly, coupled, and achieved orgasm. But it was a wordless, dusty affair that left no lingering haze of joy, and was followed by immediate sleep for him, wide-awake restlessness and a gnawing sense of loss for her. Something had been taken, or had it been withdrawn, from *her*.

The day had been a two-dimensional façade, built over a wall of white noise that filled the paper-thin gap between them. It had leeched into the fissures in Kristen's confidence, burrowed deep into her soul. The enormity of it was not muted by the façade, rather it was amplified by the mask of affection Daniel had worn.

Kristen forced herself back to the now. The report on her screen made dire reading; failures to meet timescales hidden behind clichés and management-speak, excuses made, blame apportioned.

The words tumbled into gibberish.

You should do the same Krissy... Tell Daniel to pick up his stuff and leave.

Catch or no catch, it would be for the best. She wasn't up to this...this game of give pleasure and approval, then withdraw it again and again until she was craven with the desire to please and the need for his touch.

She should claim a migraine, go back to the flat so she could be there when Daniel came home from his own office – wherever and whatever that was, he was oddly protective of his work life.

He may be there already.

God, she hadn't thought of that. His hours were unpredictable, hard to pin-down, like everything else about this relationship.

Well, if he was, at least she could get the confrontation over with.

I'm sorry Daniel, it isn't working. I can't go on with this. I would like you leave.
Now? Could he leave *now*, with no warning or discussion? Was that fair?

Kristen slumped back in the chair, skin prickling, breath reduced to short, quick gasps. She was exhausted. The day stretched out before her, infinite in its monotony, underpinned by simmering panic. She reached for the phone on her desk. "Aaron?" Her boss. "I'm really sorry, but I can feel a migraine coming on. I need to go home."

It took Kristen two hours to get back to the flat, because she shopped on the way. Once home, (no Daniel) she showered, sprayed perfume, then unbagged her purchases and dressed; red basque, stockings, all overlaid by her fur coat. She lit candles, selected schmaltzy music, painted her lips. Tramp, tart, it didn't matter. She slipped on her gleaming new scarlet heels, sat down and waited. She was soon hot and uncomfortable.

This was ridiculous, demeaning even.

Time crawled by. Candles flickered and soft music whispered. The door opened.

Daniel looked tired, his chin dark with a day's growth. He stared at her and smiled. She went to him. He kissed her.

She gave herself to him in the warm, red-lit isolation of their bedroom. She took him in her mouth. He licked her to an orgasm so intense it was if the world had shattered into a million glinting shards around her. They lay together, at peace, he murmured to her and slowly aroused her again. Kisses, this time, and touches. His tongue flickered, its impacts feather-light, an electric dance of sensation. So fast, so... snake-like.

As she drifted into the haze of her pleasures, Kristen felt him wind about her, slide over and into her. As the waves rose again, she bit down on his dust-dry skin. She could no longer move. He held her tight, wrapped, arms and legs immobile. Panic flared, only to dissolve into a glissando of metal-bright pleasure. She curled into him, seeking refuge in his strong warmth.

Then he whispered in her ear. "Why did you dress up like a whore? Is that what you think I want?"

The words sliced through her like ice. She struggled to wake, but was too far down in the grey haze to claw her way back, so she took the jagged splinter with her into sleep

He was gone when she woke. It was light, too light.

She sat up and scrabbled for her mobile phone. Ten-fifteen. Fuck! Late for work was an understatement; this was death-knell late. She became aware that she was still wearing her basque, and one stocking, crumpled about her left leg. The other was gone. Her coat and high heels were strewn across the floor.

Why did you dress up like a whore?

She felt cheap. What had been a need last night seemed tawdry and embarrassing now.

Is that what you think I want?

And what about that resolution, the reason she had left work early yesterday (and risked the ire of her manager – not known for his caring attitude)? Somehow, at some instant she could not pinpoint, it had crumbled into pure need. Kristen closed her eyes, lay back and struggled to remember when and why. She couldn't. The blank spot in the timeline frustrated then alarmed her. Why couldn't she recall the moment, the thought process? It was all darkness, a red-tinged mist.

Kristen sat up again and felt dizzy. Her head ached.

She needed to shower, dress, get to work. But she couldn't. She could barely move. Titanic effort was required for her to get to the bathroom.

The face in the mirror above the sink was ashen. Its eyes were bloodshot and dark-ringed, and not only from smudged mascara. She looked ill, which was a relief, in a way. Here was her excuse for not going into work and getting more sleep.

Why did you dress up like a whore?

Kristen made the call. Aaron was characteristically irritable.

"How long will you be off?"

"Just today. The migraine's worse. I'll try to work at home."

"All right, but keep me in the loop."

In the loop? The fucking noose, more like. Kristen went back to bed and drifted into a restless half-sleep.

And he came to her.

Her mouth was dry, her throat tight, her skin hypersensitive to his touch. She whispered his name and felt his breath hot on her belly, her groin. She felt his kisses, his tongue. Dear God, his tongue...

He was all over her, sliding and coiling and biting and touching. And all the time his tongue worked at her. Worked and worked.

This isn't right, whispered hard-arsed Kristen. *Wake-up, for Christ's sake, wake up!*

Too late for that. Too late, oh God, oh God...

Spent, Kristen reached for him. Nothing. No one. But she could smell him, feel him.

It was this fever, high temperature, hallucination. She slumped back onto the pillow, weaker than ever now. She wanted Daniel here, wanted him back. Perhaps he was still in the flat, in the kitchen, making coffee. She couldn't hear anything. But he had to be here somewhere. He couldn't just disappear.

You have to get out of this, before you go crazy.

The thought was brutal and stark.

It didn't matter that it was her flat. She could deal with ownership and eviction once she was at a safe distance. Right now, she had to leave.

Kristen crawled out of bed and over to the wardrobe. She grabbed a handful of clothes and rammed them into a suitcase then sat on the bed, exhausted. The panic was back. She picked up the phone, called Sarah.

"God Krissy, at last. I'm at work at the moment, but come to the shop and get the key to the house. There's a duvet folded up on the spare bed, and sheets and pillows in the cupboard. Make yourself at home."

Kristen resumed packing. Time was racing by. Daniel could return at any moment.

Hadn't he been home already?

Kristen struggled on, stumbled into the bathroom to scoop up her toiletries then back into the bedroom to tip them into the case. She zipped the lid and knelt beside it, breathing hard, almost panting from the exertion. Her headache beat her skull in rhythmic waves of pain. She shivered, despite the heat that radiated through her.

She needed to lay down, for a while, to recover her strength.

Mad idea, insanity. She had to get out, before Daniel came back, before he crushed her resolve with his quiet bewilderment at the idea that she would walk out on him.

Before he drew her back with his smile and his touches and his tender, electric kisses.

Gathering the remaining shreds of her strength, Kristen hauled herself to her feet and got the case up onto its wheels. She dragged it to the door, and hesitated. She looked back at the bedroom.

Their room, their refuge, the core of their pleasure. The duvet was rumpled, turned down, the mattress soft, inviting. Her whore clothes, but for the fur coat which she was wearing, were still on the floor.

Stay. Daniel will look after you, he'll surround and comfort and *smother you*

The afternoon light dropped a stage. Night was coming.

Kristen leaned against the door frame. She had to do this. Daniel was sucking the life out of her. She pressed on, made it to the flat's main door before she needed another rest. Her eyes burned, her throat was raw, every swallow a sandpaper-grate over inflamed tissue.

Out, onto the landing. She headed for the lift. The suitcase was a thousand tons, its wheels dragged through wet sand. She pressed the call button. Waited. The lift was eleven floors below her. The lift was crawling upwards. The lift was not empty. Daniel was in there. Daniel was coming.

A *ding*. A moment. Then the doors slid opened. The lift was empty. Its metal and cheap wood panel walls dented and scuffed, but empty. Kristen manoeuvred the case inside and, as the doors closed again and the lift jerked into descent, slid down to crouch in the corner, hugging herself, jaw tautened by her mounting fever tremors.

The brief yet eternal journey ended with a slight bump. The doors opened once more, this time to reveal the lobby; a sparse, utilitarian affair replete with magnolia walls and concrete stairs. The case required two hands now, and for Kristen to drag it out backwards. Every tightening of her muscles ricocheted through her temples as pain.

She shambled across the lobby to the main doors. Beyond was the short roadway that joined the flats' car park to the main street. She saw cars, light, glimpsed people. She saw rain spotting the glass. She saw cold, and desolation, and utter, relentless loneliness.

She couldn't.

She must.

Checking her coat pocket for her car keys, Kristen reached for the exit button that would unlock the door.

A car swung into the roadway and bathed her in a brief glare of headlight.

Daniel. It had to be Daniel. For a moment she was frozen, staring out at the yellow-white blaze. Daniel, home. Turning off the ignition, drawing the key from its slot. Seatbelt unlocked.

Panting now, each breath mixed with a sob, Kristen stumbled back to the lift. Someone else had called it. The thing was on its way up. Shit, fuck. No, it was descending now. Slow, so bloody slow. She glanced back at the front door. He must not catch her here with the case. She had to be ready for him.

The lift arrived. She all but fell inside. Up. He must be at the door now, punching the combination, waiting for the click of the lock.

Twelfth floor, landing, key. Where was the fucking key? Here, in her pocket. She fumbled it into the lock, and was inside the flat.

She let go of the case which tipped over behind her. She peeled off the coat and let it drop to the floor. Her sweater, dragged over her head, her blouse, buttons torn off, hurled aside. Jeans, tripped over, stepped out of. The bed. The warm place. She shivered in its hot embrace and waited.

She heard a key in the lock. The light outside faded to night-black. The light in the bedroom seemed to grey and grow dim, as if he pushed shadow before him as he moved towards the bedroom. A wave of darkness seeped into the room and kissed her long before she felt his lips descend on her skin.

Jar of Flies

(This one's for Luke)

1

There were people everywhere, strangers, swarming over the immaculate, sun-bright kitchen. One of them, a hatchet faced character in a crumpled grey suit stepped forward to block her way. "You can't come in here," he growled.

"The Millwoods are members of my congregation," the Reverend Karen Smith answered. "I...I must pray for them."

"You'll have to pray for them in your church—"

"I have to pray for them *here*." She didn't know why. The need had been on her since Myra White rang her with the news.

Hatchet Face shook his head. "I'm sorry. You need to go, this is a crime scene."

Karen made to protest again. Then saw the bodies over Hatchet Face's shoulder. A glimpse, yet intense and terrible enough to burn itself into her mind and threaten to haunt her dreams from now until end of her life.

Geoffrey Millwood, church deacon, lay on the floor. A portly middle-aged man in white-paper overalls was crouched beside him. He looked up and spoke. Hatchet Face spun round to listen, but remained in place, his back a broad, forbidding barrier that denied Karen entrance.

"Seems pretty straightforward, Chief Inspector," said the man in overalls. "Murder then suicide."

"How so?"

"Well, that wound on Millwood's throat."

Throat? Karen forced herself to look. There was a black-red hole where Geoffrey's throat should have been.

"She severed his jugular, tore out his oesophagus and trachea." The pathologist shook his head. "Christ I've never seen anything like it." He seemed to notice Karen for the first time. "Sorry..."

"It's okay." Her voice was hoarse. She had seen death before, it was part of the job, but it was invariably peaceful, illness-death. Not this flesh and blood photograph of agony and terror.

"She?" Hatchet Face, the Chief Inspector, said.

"His wife. She bit him."

And that was when Karen saw Janet.

She lay on the table amidst the wreckage of an unfinished meal. Her face was blood-masked and fly-covered. The handle of a knife protruded from her chest, rammed in so hard that no trace of blade was visible. Both her hands were clenched about the handle.

"God knows how she managed that," the pathologist said. "I mean, she rammed it in so hard she broke two ribs."

"So you're telling me that she served her husband his lunch, tore out his throat then killed herself," the Chief Inspector said.

No, not so. This was Janet Millwood, seventy-plus and sprightly Janet. Brusque-but-generous Janet, who had supported Karen's appointment to the parish and seen off all opposition with the ferocity of a lioness.

The Chief Inspector returned his attention to Karen. "How well do you know the Millwoods, Reverend?"

Karen stared at the Chief Inspector, uncomprehending. Suddenly she needed to get away...

It was the detective who caught her as she fell.

They found shade, on a bench under an ancient apple tree in the Millwood's rear garden. Bees droned, butterflies danced. "I'm sorry," Karen said. "I thought I could..."

"You did bloody well in there." The Chief Inspector said. "I was sick every time for years."

He was probably lying, but it was comforting anyway.

"I'm Chief Inspector Gant, by the way."

Karen introduced herself in return.

Gant studied her carefully. "You seem a little…"

"Young to be a vicar, especially a female vicar?"

"Well yes."

"There are plenty of traditionalists in this village who would agree with you. I'm serious about this job, Inspector; this is my life, my vocation."

"Be careful of vocations," Gant said quietly. "They break things."

"Like marriages?" She shouldn't have said it. It was none of her business.

Gant didn't seem to mind. "Tell me about the Millwoods."

"Geoffrey was reliable, an old fashioned gentleman. Janet was one of *those* people; busy, loyal, a little domineering, but a good friend to me."

"Is there anything you can think of that would have caused her to kill her husband?" Gant asked. "Anything in their lives? *Anything?*"

"No." An instinctive answer. Karen faltered, regained control.

And remembered.

"They lost a baby. Cot death, you'd call it now. They never had any other children. But it was a long time ago. Fifty years."

"Nothing," Gant said. "Is a long time ago."

2

Eight pm and, thankfully, the light was fading. The afternoon had been hell, for want of a better word. Karen now stood outside the front door of James Ward's bungalow, her knees numb, her soul empty. James was one of her predecessors as Vicar of All Saints.

The door was opened at her second knock. James Ward was frail and stooped. His smile was broad, his eyes bright. "Karen," he said. "Come in, come in."

He led her into his comfortably untidy lounge and, as always, made pretence of clearing up. This time he selected an ancient book that was lying face down on the coffee table, restoring it to its place among the ranks of similarly geriatric tomes. Karen noticed that there was also a whisky bottle and two empty tumblers on the table.

"Expecting someone?" she asked.

"I can't say I'm surprised to see you," he said as he poured, then handed Karen a glass. "Have you prayed?"

"*He* wasn't listening." She winced as the scotch burned its way down.

"He was."

"I just don't understand why this was allowed to happen...." She stopped herself. "Here comes the classic question."

James grinned. "We spend our lives telling others that suffering is a test from God, but when it happens to us we're as confused as everybody else." The grin faded. "We always blame God for Satan's work."

"You know I don't believe in the Devil. Evil comes from within man."

"My answer's the same as always, if you believe in God, you have to believe in Lucifer." James frowned, concerned now. "I'm sorry Karen, this isn't the time for theological debate."

Karen paused, then said; "There's something else."

"Something else?"

"I can't put my finger on it." Karen sipped again, and felt a little better. "I've noticed an *atmosphere* in the village. It was even affecting the Millwoods. They'd become awkward, tense. As if they were hiding something."

"They were."

"Ah, I know there's opposition–"

"It isn't about you. You've made a grand start here. If you could impress Janet Millwood, you could impress anyone."

"Poor Janet," Karen let the tears roll this time.

"The problem is Alice Rackham."

"Alice? You mean the old lady who moved into Red Farm Cottage a couple of months ago?"

"The very one. She's lived here before, was born here in fact. She had a nervous breakdown, sometime in the early sixties, ended up in a psychiatric hospital and disappeared out of our lives. Now she's suddenly reappeared. She wasn't popular, particularly with the female population. She was beautiful you see, and worse still, she was a single parent. They had other names for it back then."

"Why has she come back?"

"I really don't know, Karen, but your instincts are right; it has caused a stir among the people old enough to remember her."

"I'll pay her a visit…"

"She'll take one look at your clerical collar and slam the door in your face."

Karen's next question was interrupted by her mobile phone.

3

This time the stench was burned flesh. This time there was a crisped, strangely doll-like parody of a human body, sitting on the floor of its garage. Male, sixty-seven. Arthur Hewlett, widower and former proprietor of the Abbotsfield Village Stores. No witnesses.

There was a burned out, heat-twisted plastic petrol can lying beside him. The garage stank of fuel and fire and violent, screaming-agony death. The corpse stared through empty sockets and grinned.

Hewlett's house was a mess, ransacked. Ornaments and crockery were smashed, books torn, picture frames and photographs hurled to the floor. There was vomit and other bodily waste everywhere.

The pathology team were already at work. Gant stood to one side, eyes hard, holding no trace of the afternoon's warmth.

"You didn't get on, did you, Reverend." It wasn't a question. "Hewlett's son told us that his father was about to give up his post as church warden because of it."

Karen felt her cheeks burn. "I was always civil to him—"

"Where were you at six-thirty this evening?"

"In my flat, praying."

"Witnesses?"

"You're not seriously suggesting…?"

Gant remained impassive. And silent.

"Look, my relationship with Mr Hewlett was… difficult. He seemed to think I was going to lure the young men of the church to my bedroom. Do you include the Millwoods in my murderous rampage?"

Gant turned his attention back to the body. "Please don't leave the village for a few days, Reverend."

4

Flies, a black swirling column, hovered above the centre of the fireside rug. The rug… the room… were unfamiliar, lit, badly, by a single standing lamp in an unseen corner. The wallpaper was heavily patterned, the woodwork and furniture dark, old, heavy. There was a smell of gas and boiled cabbage. *Her* home…

Not her home.

Karen stood on the edge of the rug. A coal fire burned in the grate. The room was hot, but it was cold outside, snowing. She knew that, even though the curtains were drawn. The flies transfixed her, the swarm holding its form, spiralling faster, faster, their incessant drone growing louder.

Karen was naked. She looked down at herself, at the body, slim, like her own, but too tall, wrong. Her hair, she tugged at a strand, was long, red-brown to her fair. There was a mirror above the mantlepiece. Her breath caught in her throat as she stared at the unfamiliar, sharp-featured yet quite beautiful face reflected in its glass. The eyes were dark, the mouth a sensuous gash of red against white.

The face smiled. She felt her own respond, flesh and blood reflecting its image.

The pale body carried Karen across the rug, to the edge of the column of flies. The creatures grew frantic, drew in close and coalesced into a solid heaving mass, a shape, a figure constructed entirely of seething, roiling insects, of obese bluebottles, grey flecked houseflies and flies that gleamed metallic green.

Her hand touched a hand of flies. She felt the restless tingle of insects. She lifted her face, parted her lips to receive his… its… their kiss.

No… something in the room that shouldn't be there, lying on a table behind the figure… alarmed now, Karen made to break away, to push past the fly-man, to reach the object. His hand tightened about her wrist. She struggled, wrenched her arm back.

And suddenly there were only flies; in her mouth, clogging her nose, grinding against her eyes, choking, smothering—

Karen woke with a cry, breathing hard, shivering despite the closeness of the night, too frightened to reach for the bedside lamp. The dream slithered about her, its detail blurring into a memory of flies.

5

Alice Rackham's home was a small cottage a mile or so outside the village. It was picturesque and ivy-softened. After knocking at the front door, Karen ventured round the side and into the rear garden.

An elderly lady was kneeling beside one of the flower borders. Karen called out. "Mrs Rackham?"

The woman looked up, frowned, then lifted a hand in greeting.

"One moment, one moment," she called back cheerfully. "Takes a little bit of time to climb off the ground these days."

Karen wondered if she should offer to help, but sensed that it would hurt this sprightly woman's pride.

The woman brushed down her long skirt and pushed a stray lock out of her eyes. Her hair was pulled back into a gleaming silver ponytail, its length unusual for someone of her age.

As she approached, Karen's hand darted instinctively to her clerical collar.

"Ah," Alice Rackham said. "I shouldn't be surprised I suppose. Send you, did they? Blaming me are they?" Her voice was soft, and edged with a Suffolk accent.

Karen opened her mouth to answer, but shock choked off her words. Alice's face, though age-carved, was the one from the dream... the face in the mirror... the face *she* had worn.

"Are you alright, Karen? You look pale. Come on, come on, sit yourself down."

Alice led the way to a green metal patio-set, located at the back of the house. Once Karen was seated, Alice crouched in front of her, holding her hand. "You've had too many shocks," she said. "Seen too many things a decent human shouldn't see."

"Yes," Karen answered, vaguely. "I suppose I have."

"Sit here and rest, I'll make us some tea." And she was gone, leaving Karen to wonder how Alice knew her name and what she had seen. Not too much of a mystery, she realised; she had probably been into the village, seen her name on the notice board outside the church, heard her talked about in one of the shops.

"You said you weren't surprised to see me," Karen said when Alice returned bearing a tray laden with an ancient looking Willow Pattern tea set. "Why is that, Mrs Rackham?"

"Oh, come on, isn't it obvious?"

"All I know is that you lived here in the past."

Alice poured tea. "I was forced to leave. My health, you see."

"Why do you think people blame you for… for what happened?"

"They think I've put a curse on them. They believe I'm a witch."

A pause, then. "*Are* you a witch, Mrs Rackham?"

"What would you think if I said yes?"

"I don't believe in witchcraft, or the Devil. I believe in the power of the human mind."

"I know all about the human mind." Alice smiled. There would have been a time, Karen decided, when that smile would have caused mayhem among the male population of Abbotsfield village. "But yes, I am a witch. A bride of that Devil you don't believe in.

"I've met him you know," she continued, over Karen's startled silence. "His name is Lucifer and he can be very charming. He *is* an angel after all. And he looks nothing like a goat, believe you me." The smile became disturbingly lascivious.

"I feel as if I should have some wise words…."

"I use my gifts for healing. That's been my life's work, repairing the broken in mind and body. Not much of that life left for me now." Something like fear clouded her smile. "There's a price, my soul."

"But why did you turn to Lucifer? Why not God?"

"God? Where was He when I needed Him?" She sat back in her chair, the smile gone. "My father was killed before I was born, in some sort of drunken brawl. My mother was half mad, convinced that God was going to punish her for something she'd done. She read the bible all the time, not a word about God's love mind, just Hell and judgement. She made me hate her God. So I prayed to His enemy instead. One night, when I was thirteen, he came to me..." Alice smiled again. "I wasn't afraid. Not then.

"After my breakdown I moved to London. I was happy there, but I had to come back here before it was my turn."

"Why?"

A fly bounced lazily across the space between the two women and landed on Alice's left hand. She ignored it. "To prove to myself that I had the courage."

The fly took off, circled Alice for a moment then headed away across the garden. "They're all living souls," she murmured. "I've no reason to hurt them. More tea?"

Karen had a sermon to finish, but it was pleasant here, and she was fascinated by this woman who claimed the Devil as a husband. So she said yes, then settled back into her chair and closed her eyes as Alice reloaded the tray and headed indoors.

Garden sounds filtered in; the soft sigh of warm wind through the trees, birds, bees and the drone of...

Karen opened her eyes. There, in the background. It sounded like flies. Unnerved, she glanced round and saw nothing but flowerbeds and lawn, birds and butterflies. Yet the noise was growing louder, drumming through her head.

She pressed her fingertips to her temples. An oncoming migraine perhaps, or something worse; no, no, that was stupid. She was tired, still in shock.

Louder.

She looked about herself, searching for the source of the sound.

And saw a large wooden shed, tucked into a corner of the garden. She found herself walking towards it, forcing her way through a thickening wall of noise. The buzzing and voices beat at her, their language incomprehensible but foul. It shivered through her flesh, scratched at her skull.

Louder.

She leaned against the cool, rough wood of the shed wall, head down, eyes closed. There was no relief, nothing but noise, black-flecked, restless, manic. She stumbled round to the door and pulled it wide.

Sound slammed into her.

She forced herself into the roaring, gibbering, aural hell. She grabbed at the edge of a workbench for support. There were shelves, laden with brown bottles, carefully labelled; "Geranium", "Star of Bethlehem", "Arnica".

And another jar, big, clear and containing a blizzard of frantic black shapes.

Flies.

Bouncing off the glass, hurling themselves against the gauze that was elastic-banded tightly over the jar's mouth.

The voices became a storm, Karen staggered back, gasping for breath, retching, gagging, disorientated, unable to see the exit...

"Be quiet!"

The buzzing stopped, the voices vanished.

Karen spun round to see Alice standing in the doorway. Her face was creased into black rage. Her eyes burned.

"Get out. Go away, leave us alone."

6

Anything but write: stare out of the window, stare at the screen of her laptop, wander round the flat, finger the spines of the books that obscured one whole wall of the tiny lounge.

The sermon was hard to construct because it required a delicate balance of sensitivity, comfort and truth. Suddenly Karen realised that she didn't know her congregation. They had lives and histories she could never penetrate. They were strangers.

She dragged her attention to the screen; electronic hieroglyphics on the grey-white background. It wasn't laziness, or the Saturday afternoon heat. It was Alice Rackham. It was that jar of flies, it was a village cowering in fear, waiting for the third death they were sure would happen.

A flick of the mouse and she was typing "witch" into a search engine. There were countless links, much of it the usual dross, but here and there...

"European witchcraft... involves a diabolical pact in which a soul is exchanged... supernatural aid can be invoked either to visit death or calamity upon enemies... Witches often possess "familiar spirits", usually animals, willing to perform any service needed."

Insects were animals. Flies were animals–

No.

Alice Rackham was an eccentric old lady who had been treated for psychiatric illness. Nothing more.

Karen's phone warbled.

"Hello, Karen," said James Ward.

"Hi, James."

"I've been worried about you."

Karen hesitated, then said; "I went to see Alice Rackham this morning."

"You did?"

"She told me she was a witch."

"Ah, yes. I didn't get a chance to warn you about that."

"Do you believe her?"

A pause. "Yes I do, Karen."

"So, do *you* think she's responsible for what happened to the Millwoods and Arthur Hewlett?"

"*I* don't, but there are some who do. Look, oddly enough, you've made the purpose of my phone call a little easier."

"Oh?"

"Well, as I said, people are upset and frightened. They've asked me to hold a special prayer meeting in the church hall tomorrow, after evensong. Would you mind? It's meant as no disrespect to you, but they *have* known me for a long time."

"Of course I don't mind. Would you like some moral support?"

"No, no thank you. I think the people involved would be happier to keep it within their own circle."

"I understand. God bless, James." God? Wasn't He a supernatural being, like Lucifer?

She needed a walk, to clear her mind. Karen grabbed her handbag, opened it, checked that she had her door keys. And froze. The dream, the table in the strange room, on the other side of the Fly Man, there had been a key on it. An ancient looking object, pitted, rusting.

7

The sermon was not her best. The ideas it contained felt disjointed, clichéd, predictable. Yet afterwards, as she took her place in the dazzling midday sunshine outside the church, she received nothing but compliments from her congregation. Any comfort, it seemed, was welcome at the moment...

"Reverend!" A familiar figure was half running, half stumbling up the path towards her.

It was Michael Warner, a gaunt, weather-lined, retired farmer. He lurched to a halt in front of her, grabbing at a lichen-encrusted headstone for support, breathing hard.

"They made me do it," he shouted. His voice was hoarse.

"Michael," Karen made to take his arm. "What's wrong?"

He shrank back, wild-eyed. "No! You mustn't touch me."

People had stopped to watch, on the path, in the porch. Karen noticed Myra White hovering nearby, ashen-faced.

Michael dropped to his knees, sobbing helplessly now. "I killed her."

"Killed?" Myra White closed in, her voice full of panic. "Killed who?"

"My Sheila. I strangled her."

Myra uttered a moan and stumbled back, covering her face. "Oh God... Oh God..."

"Michael," Karen said as quietly, as calmly, as she could. "Are you telling me that you... that you killed your wife?"

"She deserved it, the bitch." Michael hissed and the tears were gone and there was hate in his eyes. "Just like the Millwoods did. Just like we all do."

"I think you'd better stay right there, Michael," Karen said carefully. She caught the eye of a younger member of the rapidly gathering crowd and mimed the word "Police". The man hurried away, drawing a mobile phone from his pocket.

"Strangling isn't easy," Michael had become sullen, resentful. "She scratched and kicked for bloody ages."

He was suddenly on his feet, as if wrenched upright by invisible hands. He grabbed at Karen's vestments, jerked her to himself. She cried, slapped at his face. Others were on him clawing and tugging, but his grip never loosened.

"Fucking Warner," he growled, only it wasn't Michael but a multitude, gurgling venom from his throat. "Fucking Millwoods. Fucking Hewlett."

He laughed, a roar of sound that contained howls and screams as well as a filthy-sounding mirth. Then he vomited, splattering foulness over Karen's vestments and into her face. And flies, a bloated, buzzing swarm that erupted from the mess and boiled out of Michael's open mouth. As Karen lifted her hands to protect herself, Michael swept a knife from his trouser pocket.

There was blood.

8

Chief Inspector Gant said nothing for a long while, but stood over the body, batting half-heartedly at the last of the flies. After a long while, he helped Karen off her knees. She had been praying since it happened, unable to stop, despite the filth and blood sprayed over her robes and hair.

"So he came to you to confess," Gant said. "Then cut his own throat."

"I don't know," Karen was terrified by her own calmness. "He... He was blaming someone..."

Flies, there had been flies...

He was demon-possessed. Like Janet Millwood had been when she ripped out her husband's throat, and Arthur Hewlett, when he vandalised his own home before lighting that match.

No. No, no, *no*.

There had been flies.

Gant shook his head. "Well he wasn't lying about his wife. She put up one hell of a fight." His expression softened. "Look Reverend, I'll get a constable to take you home."

"No..." She couldn't leave that body. It was another of her people; a gentle, generous man who had worked hard all his life, a father, a husband.

"The pathologist is waiting; we can't leave Warner out here all afternoon." His hand was on her arm, gentle. "There'll be no evening service. We'll need to seal off the church for a while."

9

Fire, smoke. She coughed, gasped for breath but there was only pain. She was bent almost double, her diaphragm crushed, her arms wrenched up behind her. She was screaming. She couldn't stop screaming. Her throat was raw with it.

Her wrists were bound and she was hanging from a tree, bare toes scrabbling for purchase on icy grass. A gust of cold air smacked her face, danced over her. She wore... a nightdress... It was wet. She was wet. The wetness stank... petrol. Dear God, petrol. It didn't matter. The burning mattered, the rage of flame and smoke where something was dying. Her screams broke into sobs, uncontrollable, hysterical. Figures were gathered round her, night-cloaked, chanting. One stepped forward. Muffled in a coat, trilby pulled over a face half in shadow, half illumed by the flames. Familiar... couldn't remember... couldn't think...

A scrape, a flare, a match.

Do it you bastard... DO IT!

Someone else now, breaking through the chanting angry shadows, knocking the match-man aside, tugging at the ropes and knots. He was dark, faceless. He buzzed and droned. He was made of flies... She felt them on her, crawling, scuttling over her petrol-drenched flesh as he worked. And... beyond the figure... on the grass and lit by flames... a table, and on the table, an ancient, rusting key...

Karen must have cried out because the PC Gant had assigned to her was in the bedroom doorway, asking if she was okay. Karen sat up, muttered about bad dreams, then asked for a coffee.

"No problem." The PC said. "I could do with one myself."

Karen moved fast, pulling on a tee shirt and jeans and checking her handbag for car keys as she tiptoed to the door. Ashamed at her deception, she slunk out through the tiny passage and into the sitting room where she grabbed one of the older books from her shelf. Then it was hall and stairs, trying not to run, or turn back, because suddenly, she was afraid.

It was raining by the time Karen came within sight of Alice's cottage. She hid her battered old hatchback in a field gateway and retrieved the light waterproof jacket she kept in the boot. The rain fell steadily, a deluge of warm tears that did nothing to relieve the oppressive heat. Thunder rumbled in the distance.

Karen picked her way carefully along the side of Alice's house. She paused at the entrance to the back garden, shivering now. No sign of Alice. Karen hurried across the lawn, angling away from the house itself, making for the shed. The trembling grew worse.

She caught her breath, then drew out the book she had taken from her shelf. It was the 1619 *Rituale Romanum* of Pope Paul V. Karen opened it at the ritual of exorcism.

Attempting to keep the book dry she tried the shed door; unlocked, like last time. She went inside, moving through the near dark, past the shelves, the brown bottles, to the glass jar, which was a grey smudge in the shadow. She reached towards it, meaning to carry it to the window where there would be enough light for her to read by...

Something was wrong, the gauze lid... gone. Dear God, she was too late...

A flash of lightning briefly illuminated the interior of the shed, and the jar. Karen moved quickly to the window and held the container up to the light.

The flies were heaped in the bottom; dead.

There was another flare of lightning. A movement. Karen spun round.

Alice, once more in the shed doorway, wild-eyed, dishevelled, a kitchen knife in her hands. Karen froze, waiting for the attack. Seconds passed. Alice stayed where she was, breathing hard, clutching the doorframe as if for support.

"Alice," Karen said softly.

The blade wavered, then arced slowly downwards until Alice was standing, shoulders slumped, knife by her side. She looked old and tired.

Alice began to cry. Karen made to go to her, but she backed away. "You can't help me. No one can."

"I can try. Please, Alice."

"I've made my choice; there's no going back."

"No one is lost. God is love—"

"It's not God I'm afraid of." She slumped forward. Karen moved quickly to catch her. Alice was a frail bag of bones. Karen lowered her to the floor, where she sat, leaning against one of the workbench legs.

"I've been having chest pains all afternoon. It's my time. *He's* coming for me. And I'm frightened, Karen." She paused for breath. "I let them go."

"The flies?"

"They've served me well over the years, been good companions. They've never harmed anyone. Never. People used to come to me, respectable people, sneaking around in the night, offering me money to hurt their enemies, even make them die. I always sent them away. That isn't why I choose this path. I only wanted comfort, I only wanted someone to look after me. I'm not evil Karen…"

"We should pray for your soul, Alice. I'll stay with you all night if necessary."

Alice laughed, a humourless, bitter sound. "You're just like Jim."

"Jim?"

"The Reverend James Ward."

Karen was startled. Of course James would have visited Alice.

"I remember him coming to the village as if it was yesterday. Middle of the 'fifties it was. He was an army chaplain, Korea, war hero. He'd been decorated for crawling out under fire to pray with a dying soldier." She sighed. "We… we formed a relationship."

"Ah."

"No, no you don't understand. It was a… a rivalry. He saw it as his mission to rid Abbotsfield of its witch. He was sincere, close to his God. My familiars were just as afraid of him as they were of you. I think he dreamed dreams the way you do. Oh yes, I know about your dreams.

Never be afraid of them. Sleepers are taken to places, shown things...

"Jim wanted to know what I believed in. He even borrowed some of my books, the *Pseudomonarchia Daemonum*, oh, and my *Lesser Key of Solomon*.

"We argued, debated and talked, but before long we weren't talking about God and Lucifer anymore."

Alice paused. There were tears. "I'd known men before; I had a child by one of the bastards, a daughter I named Ellen after my grandmother. But none of them were fit to lick Jim's shoes.

"We tried to keep it secret, but this is a village." Alice paused to catch her breath. "Someone from the church found out. There was a panic. Jim was forced to make a choice, God or love..." She flared, momentarily. "I spit on his God, on any God who is so cruel He tears lovers apart."

The anger dissolved into quiet weeping. Karen covered Alice's limp, cold hands with her own.

"The Millwoods were the ring leaders. They were young then, self-righteous and as hard as nails. They had a baby. A week or so after they made Jim turn his back on me, the baby died. They claimed that I'd cursed the child...

"Then they came for me late one night. I was befuddled because I was using herbs to sleep, by the time I realised what was happening..."

Glass shatters... Footsteps on the stairs. A child cries...

"I staggered out onto the landing, straight into the arms of two men. Someone else was..."

Backing out of Ellen's bedroom, splashing the contents of a can over the floor. It's a woman, young, but familiar. She straightens, turns and it is Janet Millwood. Janet puts the can down and produces a box of matches.

"I struggled and pleaded with her. But she just stared at me, cold, like a dead body, then struck a match and threw it into Ellen's room."

They twist her arms behind her as they all stumble down the stairs away from the smoke and terrible, terrible heat. She... Karen... Alice... is screaming, her throat raw. Outside, it's cold, dark, yet light. There are people. Faces unmasked by the brightening orange fury. Myra White, Arthur Hewlett, Michael Warner and his plump little wife Mary. Then someone ties her wrists, roughly, tightly and, still screaming, she is dragged towards the ash tree by the gate...

"I only remember that I wanted to die. I wanted Geoffrey Millwood to light that match..."

Do it you bastard... Do it... DO IT!

"Then Jim came." Alice chuckled. "Descended on them like Moses from Mount Sinai."

The Fly Man... knocking Geoff Millwood aside, tugging at knots and ropes. The Fly Man... James Ward... Jim... and the key... behind him... The key...

"He even borrowed some of my books..."

James Ward, on Friday night, removing only *one* book from the clutter on his coffee table when Karen visited... key... the *Lesser Key of Solomon...*

"My God," Karen uttered, and it was no blasphemy.

10

Karen drove fast, crunching gears, cornering by instinct.

She had left Alice, sitting in her shed, fading as fast as the storm-smeared daylight. That's what Alice had wanted, she had been adamant. Karen must get to the church hall. She would not die alone... The thought turned Karen's soul to ice.

There had been one phone call. To Chief Inspector Gant.

Light spilled round an oncoming bend. Van.

A desperate wrench on the wheel and the car juddered against the verge. Light, noise, a hell of bouncing and the deafening blast of a horn. Branches slapped the windscreen.

Then storm-darkness and driving rain, and a rear view mirror, smeared bloody by the van's tail lights.

The road wound on, distance distorted, the day darkening too quickly, as if something vast and malevolent had shrouded the tattered remains of the lowering sun. Karen had never been afraid of the dark before, but she was afraid of *this* dark. She attempted prayer. The words were dust in her mouth.

His face tight with anger, Chief Inspector Gant clambered from his own car, which was parked outside the redbrick simplicity of Abbotsfield church hall, and ran to Karen's, shouting at her as she climbed out into the rain. Why had she taken it into her head to disappear? No she wasn't under arrest, and no, she wasn't a suspect, but for God's sake, she had just witnessed a bloody suicide, she was... was... Words failed him.

"Come inside with me," she said.

Trusting in his gruff protectiveness, Karen strode towards the hall's main entrance. She grasped the handle and pulled. Eyes closed, she silently cried out to her God.

James Ward's congregation was mixed, the older element Karen had expected, liberally sprinkled with their younger relatives and other church members innocent of any crime against Alice Rackham. They were on their feet, hymn singing to Myra White's piano accompaniment. James Ward himself was standing on the stage, clutching his hymn book in one hand, his walking stick in the other.

No one paid Karen more heed than a turned head and friendly nod.

Heart thundering, Karen opened the *Rituale Romanum* for the second time that day. She took a deep breath then set off up the aisle between the chairs. As she walked, she read. Her voice, though raised, sounded small against the singing.

"I exorcise thee most vile spirits," she shouted. "In the name of Jesus Christ, get out and flee this place. He Himself commands you..."

The hymn faltered, people stared, puzzled, bemused.

Gant grabbed Karen's arm, she shrugged him off, kept her eye fixed on the mould-speckled page of the old book. "Why dost thou stand and resist when thou knowest that Christ the Lord will destroy thy strength?"

"Stop it!" James shouted above the collapsing hymn. "You don't know what you're doing."

"I adjure thee, thou old serpent, by the judge of the quick and dead that thou and thine own depart immediately..."

"These murdering bastards deserve to suffer for what they did to her," James yelled. "They burned her child!"

The atmosphere tightened.

"...from this place. Yield therefore..."

With surprising agility, James swept something from behind the stage curtain with his stick. Lightning flashed, the lights dipped. It was a huge jar, rolling towards the front of the stage. The jar faltered then tumbled over the edge.

Glass shattered.

Karen's voice became more urgent. Something else was speaking through her now. "Yield therefore not to Christ," she exclaimed. "Let the name of God be terrible unto thee..."

There was a loud buzzing. Darkness swirled up from the wreckage of the jar, coalesced then erupted outwards. Flies, a thousand flies, swept over the heads of the panic-frozen congregation.

The buzzing became laughter, a deafening, reverberating insanity of voices. Karen felt them pound into her skull, felt them caress and penetrate.

"Let the name of God be terrible to thee!" she shouted, voice hoarse. "For it is God who commands thee!"

There were screams, someone on the floor, convulsing, foaming at the mouth, spine arched. Someone else was on his knees, shaking his grey-salted head like an insane rock fan, spraying spittle, vomit, howling curses. All this to the maniac piano accompaniment beaten out of the instrument as Myra White hammered her forehead rhythmically against the keys.

And everywhere flies, clogging nostrils, careering into madness-opened mouths.

"Go therefore thou transgressors. Tremble and flee at the name of the Lord." Something was building inside Karen. Something awful that threw back her head and roared from her throat. "In His name depart. Depart. DEPART!"

The voices became a howl of pain as the flies rose in a cloud that spiralled into the darkness above the light fittings. There was a cry, an explosion of black that hurtled outwards, shattering every window in the hall. Then silence, but for the moans of the injured and a brief dry rain of insect corpses.

The doors burst open, uniforms spread quickly through the chaos. Radios crackled, orders were given.

Exhausted, Karen finished her journey to the stage, where James now lay clutching at his chest.

"Alice?" James groped feebly for her hand. He slumped back, frowning, staring through her, as if seeing something she couldn't. He smiled. But there was also fear. "Alice... I'm coming..."

Karen started as someone, some*thing* touched her. She spun round and saw... a shadow, vast, terrible, beautiful. Then nothing. When she turned back James Ward was still, his face locked in a rictus of pain... and terror.

She knelt to pray, but knew it was too late. After a while, there was another touch, Gant, hand on her shoulder. He kept it there, even when she covered his hand with hers.

HISTORICAL FOOTNOTE: *In Vienna, in 1538, Jesuit exorcists claimed to have expelled 12,652 demons from a 16 year old girl. The girl blamed her grandmother for her possession, claiming that she had been keeping the demons as flies in a jar. A confession of witchcraft was tortured out of the unfortunate old lady and she was burned to death.*

(From *Binding the Devil: Exorcism Past and Present* by Roger Baxter, Arrow Books, 1975 edition)

THE DEVIL'S EGGS

(For Judy, with thanks for her encouragement)

The battered, rust-blotched minibus slowed to a halt a few yards from where Khaled waited. Its single working rear lamp spilled bloody light into the swirl of icy mist. Just like home, Khaled thought as he took a last drag at his Marlboro. There were a lot of vehicles like that in Afghanistan.

Khaled ground the dog-end under the heel of his trainer. The shoes were borrowed, as were his jeans, thick sweater and hooded coat. They belonged to his cousins who were sheltering him here in England. He would find a place of his own as soon as he could. But first he needed money, which was why, after a furtive glance up and down the deserted street, he set off towards the van.

A round, unshaven face looked out at him from the rolled-down driver's window. Another man sat beside the driver, features indistinct in the small-hours gloom.

"Are you Billy?" Khaled had been briefed to ask the question.

"That's me, now get in."

All the van's tattered, foam-bleeding seats were taken. Two people squatted on the litter-strewn metal floor. Khaled sighed and squeezed himself down beside them. Some of the passengers slept, heads rested on folded jackets, others quietly conversed with friends.

Khaled heard no Afghan spoken, but no English either. Most, if not all of his new companions, he guessed, were in this country illegally – just like him.

As the van rattled out of the town, Khaled became aware that his neighbour was a young woman. The forced intimacy made him nervous. Such contact would be unthinkable at home. Khaled's stolen glances revealed a contemptuous, pale face and long, thick dark hair. She hugged a worn, metal-studded leather jacket about herself and seemed sunk, deep, into some far-off place.

Khaled pulled his Marlboros from inside his coat. After a moment's hesitation, he offered the pack to the girl. Her eyes widened and contempt was replaced by a smile.

"Thanks," she said, placing a cigarette between her lips. She was British, which startled Khaled. He thought that only illegals like himself worked for these so-called manpower agencies.

"My pleasure," he said. "My name is Khaled by the way."

"I'm Dawn," she replied. "You speak good English,"

"My father taught me."

They smoked in companionable silence as the van creaked and roared and the sun turned the darkness grey.

The journey ended in the entrance to a bleak, fog-drenched field.

Billy banged the vehicle's flanks. "Come on you lazy bastards, out! Schnell! Schnell!"

The workers, revealed in the pale light as a mixture of East European, Arabic and a handful of Chinese, huddled together, muttering and shivering, all under the watchful eye of Billy's mate. His name, according to Dawn, was Mike. He was stocky, like Billy, with the same close-shaved scalp, but there was a gleam of malicious intelligence in his iron-hard eyes. He carried a shotgun, rested in the crook of his arm. The weapon's barrels were cut short. The sight of the gun, and the man's casual familiarity with it, struck ice into Khaled's soul. How many men had he seen with such weapons in their hands and wearing that same, coldly superior smile?

"Right," Billy shouted, "Get those spades and sacks out of the van so we can start digging." He turned to Dawn. "Feeling lucky, gorgeous?"

He set off across the field, Dawn beside him and the rest of the work gang strung out in his wake. Mike followed some distance behind, as if to pick off any stragglers.

Dawn slowed, hugged herself; Khaled saw that she was trembling. At first he thought it was the raw cold, but the tremors grew worse.

"What is wrong with her?" he asked. "She is ill—"

"Shut up and let her concentrate," Billy snapped back at him.

Breathing hard, Dawn took a few more paces then pointed at the ground. "There."

Billy grinned at Khaled. "Right, Ali Barber, you can go first."

"What are we looking for?" Khaled asked him.

"The Devil's Eggs." Billy laughed. "Now get on with it. And don't bloody break any."

Khaled watched the work party move on then lit himself a cigarette. He glanced nervously about the field. This was a bad place.

He began to dig, carefully, as instructed. The soil was dark and heavy, sprinkled with lush weeds that gave an impression of neglect. His first half-dozen spadefuls turned up nothing and he began to wonder if he was the butt of some joke.

But no, there, something, white and smooth, glimpsed then lost in an avalanche of upturned earth. Khaled laid the spade on the ground and scraped away the tumbled soil until, once again, white showed through. The object was warm, soft-fleshed and roughly spherical, about the size of a grapefruit. He slid his hands about it and was startled to find that the sphere was warm.

This, then, must be one of the Devil's Eggs.

Khaled gently scraped around the general area with his spade and quickly unearthed another egg. Three more followed, but a wider search of his patch revealed no more. He called out to Billy, who trotted over, looked into Khaled's sack and grinned. "Five of the little bastards! Not bad for a beginner. Come on, Dawnie's found another clutch."

They stopped at midday. The sky, which had turned a bright winter blue that morning, was beginning to cloud. A cold breeze had sprung up. The gang sat in the minibus, Dawn on the vehicle's back step. She smoked but didn't eat.

Khaled gathered his courage and went to sit beside her. He offered her some of his food.

"No thanks."

"But you work so hard."

She chuckled. "What I fancy is ice cream."

Khaled frowned. "Ice cream? *Today?*" He shook his head. "Come, eat, please."

"You don't give up do you?" She shrugged and nibbled at the black bread and goat's cheese he had handed to her. She was shaking.

"Cold?"

"No."

"Perhaps you are weak because you haven't eaten."

"Yeah, maybe." She looked at him, exhaled cigarette exhaust. "Why're *you* here then?"

"To earn money. To make a better life."

"I really can't eat this." Dawn handed the bread and cheese back. "It was nice of you though." Her eyes softened and she smiled. "You're not telling me the truth, are you, Khaled."

Her directness startled him into answering.

"My father was murdered, and I was next."

"Jesus, I'm sorry. It's none of my business..."

"He was an educated man, a teacher." The words were spilling out, unstoppable, like anger. "He taught tolerance and compassion. He even educated my three sisters and told them that they were free to marry who they wanted. Then the Taliban came to power. They closed his school and ordered him to stay silent. He did not believe in silence...

"When the Taliban were defeated, the Americans told us that democracy was coming and we believed that we were free. Democracy!" Khaled spat out the word. "Our village came under the authority of a Northern Alliance warlord who had coveted the region for many years. Now he had us and it was worse than the Taliban days. I was of age and wanted to re-open my father's school and carry on with his work. The warlord forbade it. I argued. He ordered me killed, so I ran away. I have not my father's courage."

Dawn touched his hand, briefly and gently. The tenderness of the act stung tears into Khaled's eyes.

"Now I have a question," he said. "How do you know where the eggs are?"

Dawn glanced over her shoulder. "I just know. So leave it at that, okay?"

In the afternoon the wind strengthened, the sky darkened prematurely, matching Khaled's mood. Telling his story to Dawn had made him homesick and ashamed. He had run like a dog. His father never ran away. Gentle as he was, he had the courage of a lion.

Khaled crouched to gather another harvest of eggs.

A shriek ripped through the wind-seared gloom. Khaled looked round wildly. There were shouts now, and sobs. He hefted the spade as a weapon and ran.

"Jesus, Jesus, oh my God..." Dawn, over and over again.

"Shut up. Shuddup you stupid bitch!" That was Billy. Khaled could see them now, and others, running like himself, dark shapes in the gloom. There was a struggle, the sharp report of a slap and Dawn stumbled back, holding her face. Enraged, Khaled drove forward and lifted the spade. Dawn began to scream his name. Screaming for him to stop. Billy spun about, huge, hulking.

A flash, a detonation and Mike was somehow between Khaled and Billy, the shotgun pointed skywards. Smoke curled from one of the barrels. Mike lowered the weapon until it was aimed at Khaled's chest.

"Go back to work," Mike's voice was quiet. "Nothing's happened. Got that? Nothing."

~

Someone was missing on the journey home. Khaled was not sure who. He thought it might be one of the Arabs.

Dawn was silent, lost to him. She sat on the van floor as before, head down, shaking violently. Khaled left her alone. Night pressed at the windows. No one spoke, all were shrunk into themselves.

A news bulletin interrupted the harsh cacophony of pop music on the radio; a Cabinet Minister's resignation, and reports of a civil war massacre in an African village.

The van lumbered to a halt and Billy shouted, "Your stop, Ali Barber!"

Khaled pushed open the rear door. Dawn laid a hand on his arm.

"Thanks Khaled" she whispered. "For being kind to me."

Then he was out into the orange-lit, damp-cold street, where Billy paid his wages, in cash.

"Tomorrow?" he snapped.

"Tomorrow," Khaled answered.

Once in his borrowed room, Khaled counted the money.

He was stunned. There must have been a mistake. Then he remembered the scream, the missing man, and Mike, with his cold, killer-eyes. The work was well paid because it was dangerous.

Khaled looked at the pile of notes again. Perhaps one more day.

He hid the cash and lay back on the bed. His hosts were downstairs, cooking the evening meal. There was music, muffled but familiar enough to stir pain-sharpened memories of his real home. For all its troubles, Afghanistan was an open, noisy and sociable world, not like Britain, where everyone isolated themselves in their houses and barely spoke to anyone else, even in the streets outside. Yet he sensed that this was a good place at heart. He just needed to find that heart.

He thought of Dawn and wanted her. She was no decent Moslem girl. She was shameless in the way she spoke. But she was in pain and he wanted to hold and comfort her... ah, it was impossible.

Why?

Was *he* of the faith? He attended to his prayers, yes, fasted during Ramadan, but did he *believe*?

~

Early the next morning Khaled once more clambered into the minibus, and was disappointed to find Dawn on a seat and made inaccessible by another passenger who was asleep beside her. The radio crackled more news of the African massacre, and comments on the similarities between this and two recent atrocities in a former Soviet republic

As with yesterday, Khaled was given the first site that Dawn found. Her trembling was worse and she kept her face averted from him.

The fog closed in, deadening all sound, isolating him in a cocoon of featureless grey that nurtured memories of the scream until it became an act of will just to force the spade into the dank, dark earth.

He wiped sweat out of his eyes then pushed the implement carefully into the next layer. Down, down...

There, an egg. He crouched, reached for it, flinched back, then grabbed the object—

"What's the matter with you then?"

Startled, Khaled snapped up his head to see Mike. He was rolling himself a cigarette.

"You did alright yesterday." Mike's smile seemed genuine enough. "You foreign bastards know how to work, I'll give you that. Khaled Khan, that's your name isn't it? Khan from 'stahn." The smile faded from Mike's eyes, though not from his mouth. "Just one thing, and I'll let you off this time because you weren't to know, don't get too friendly with Dawnie, okay?"

"Why?"

The smile vanished. "You ask too many questions. Just keep your hands off her. She might be made for sharing, but you can't afford her, right?"

"I understand."

Mike patted his shoulder, pushed the cigarette between his lips and wandered away.

Khaled dug. The unease returned. He glanced towards Dawn, who was strolling systematically back and forth across the field. Khaled tore his eyes away and stabbed the spade viciously into the ground.

There was a squelch and a tiny shriek that rebounded through his skull until it was a deafening howl of terror. Fists pressed to his temples, he peered into the pit he had dug and saw the ruin of an egg, sliced in two by his spade.

Something writhed in the mess of viscous yellow fluid; white-grey and worm-like, a foot or so long. He saw legs and pincers.

Soil exploded upwards, and glimpsed in the heart of the blinding gout of earth was a living, writhing vastness, huge and alive and utterly and completely terrifying.

Khaled screamed in Afghan, suddenly unable to remember any English. Screamed and screamed as something glutinous and tentacle-like lashed itself about his right ankle—

There was a bang, ichors sprayed Khaled's face and his leg jerked free. He was still screaming, the sound driven from him by a fear so primal it was animal and all-but incomprehensible. Then Dawn was trying to drag him away from the dig. Others arrived; rough hands snagged his arms and wrenched him backwards.

Billy appeared next, face white with rage, fists clenched. "I told you to be careful. I told you, I bloody told you!"

Finally there was Mike, the smoking shotgun in his right fist. "Okay Billy, hey, calm down mate. I'll sort it." Billy turned away and began browbeating the others back to work. Mike closed on Khaled until his face was a mere few inches away. "Too busy leering at the lovely Dawn, weren't you? This is your last warning; one more cock-up and you'll be dealt with."

~

At last, long after dark, Khaled was heading home. Dawn once again had a window seat. Khaled's stop came. He received his pay then watched the van disappear round the corner. There was a moment of debilitating loneliness and fear. He was already wondering how he had managed to keep going through the day after his own *incident*.

Whatever had come for him out of the earth had been burned. The scorched-flesh stench of the bonfire had lingered on the fog-smothered air for hours.

In a hurry to get home now, Khaled shoved his hands into his coat pockets and set off at a brisk pace. His fingers brushed something unfamiliar. Puzzled, he drew out a square of cardboard, emblazoned on one side with a crest and the word "Adnams". The card was battered and marred by a circular stain. He turned it over. "Red Lion – Tonight" was written in a spidery, shaky hand.

What was a Red Lion? Another look at the Adnams crest, and he saw the words "Broadside" and "strong ale". Ah, now he understood.

Puzzled, he tucked the card back into his pocket and headed for home. He was tense, nervous of the dark and shadow. His mind ran and reran the attack. He couldn't go back tomorrow. He must find other work.

He rounded the corner into his street, and stopped. Suddenly he didn't want to go home. There was too much time to think there.

~

Unsure of what you did in such a place, Khaled forced himself to step over the threshold into the Red Lion. Crowded with raucous, noisy humanity, both male and female, it seemed at once welcoming and hostile. A huge television displayed a jungle village, glimpses of bodies, a reporter speaking of terrible atrocities. The noise and the warmth overwhelmed him and his head began to swim.

Then he saw her, huddled at a corner table, a bottle of beer untouched in front of her. Khaled hurried over and slid into the seat opposite. Dawn looked up at him, her face gaunt and pale.

"Thank God." She rubbed furiously at red-rimmed eyes with her leather sleeve and Khaled realised that she was crying. "I bought you a beer."

He made to refuse, then, not wanting to offend her, took up the bottle and drank from it. The liquid was bitter, cold and unpleasant.

"I have to get away," Dawn said. "Before it kills me."

"Kills you?"

"It happened to the last of their egg-searchers. She went crazy and OD'd. Those creatures mess your head up. I have to go tonight, I know too much. If Mike finds out he'd…"

"I thought he loved you."

Dawn laughed. "He's my pimp, you idiot." She reached across the table, a sudden, surprising motion, and took his hands. Hers were warm and soft, and shaking. "You asked me how I know where the Eggs are. Some of us can *feel* them. I think they feel me too."

"What are they?"

She shuddered. "I don't know. I don't care."

"But you said that you *know* too much."

A pause, she glanced at the door, as if expecting someone, then returned her attention to Khaled. "There are two types, male and female, I suppose. One type lives underground and lays the eggs. That was what attacked you, and took that poor bastard yesterday. The other kind… You saw, when you broke the egg. They're what we're harvesting."

"What for?"

"I swear to you, I don't know." She pushed the bottle into his hands. "You look as if you need some more of this."

Khaled drank, realising that he was feeling pleasantly dizzy.

Another glance entrance-wards. "Where the hell *is* he?"

"Who?"

"Another piece of scum. Everyone I meet is a bastard." Her eyes softened and her voice dropped to a whisper. "Except you." Tears brightened Dawn's eyes. "You've got to get away as well."

"I have nowhere to go."

"Nor do I, but I'm going there anyway." A third look towards the entrance. She stiffened. "It's him." There was an odd hunger in her eyes as she stood up. "Look, get yourself away, okay. Go anywhere, but don't stay in this town. And don't follow me."

Before Khaled could protest or ask any more questions, Dawn was hurrying towards a figure who loitered by the door. It was a man, tall, keeping to the shadows. Khaled felt a pang of jealousy, especially when she took his arm and allowed him to take her outside. He swigged the beer, uncertain what to do. The stink of alcohol, sweat and perfume, the roar of conversation and loud laughter pounded at his senses. He lurched to his feet, wavered a little, then rushed for the exit.

The Red Lion stood on a junction, abutted to a busy, bright-lit main street. The feeder road was narrow and ill-lit, pocked with dark doorways and alley-mouths. Instinct told him that was where Dawn had gone. He walked, slowly, peering into the night-splashed niches and entrances.

And heard voices, one feminine, the other gruff and male. Khaled stopped. A tall figure detached itself from a shop doorway and slipped away.

Khaled moved quickly.

"Dawn?"

"Jesus!" She sounded terrified. "Go away you idiot!"

Khaled swung into the doorway and grabbed her arms. "I want to you to come with me."

"No, I can't."

He pulled her to himself and she fought, briefly, before subsiding against him. He felt her shaking and knew she was crying again. He stroked her hair, which smelled of cigarettes and stale perfume but was deliciously soft beneath his hand. "This is terrible, giving yourself to men..."

"No. I wasn't... He wasn't..." She pulled away. "See this? Huh? See it?" She held out her hand; a small plastic bag lay on her palm. Though the light was bad, Khaled could see the white powder it contained. "This is what he was all about, and it's why we can't stay together. I'll slow you down. I'll be forever looking for my next fix."

"I ran away from my family," Khaled answered her. "I betrayed my father's memory. I will not desert you."

~

They caught a bus and headed out into the countryside. It was a random choice. Dawn was asleep, head resting on Khaled's shoulder.

Time passed, half an hour, an hour, the bus swaying and droning. Khaled's eyes grew heavy.

Suddenly Dawn sat up and stabbed her finger into the bell push. A few minutes later the bus slowed and stopped. The doors hissed open and they found themselves on a grassy bank watching the vehicle trundle away. The moon was full, the sky clear. The entrance to a side-road lay a few yards to their left. The side-road led, in turn, to a distant twinkle of lights.

"Probably a village," Dawn said. "Let's head that way for a start."

They found the barn long before they reached the village. It was a broken down wooden structure that looked as if it had been on the verge of collapse for decades. Its big main door wasn't locked and it seemed reasonably dry inside. There was a smell of grease and oil; its source, several large cans of diesel or petrol piled carelessly against one wall. By the glow of Dawn's lighter they noticed a smaller back door and saw that one half of the building was piled with straw bales. Better still, there was a convenient hiding place between the rear of the stack and the barn wall.

"I hope there's no spiders," Dawn muttered. "I hate spiders."

Once settled into the straw, Khaled enfolded Dawn in his arms. The action was natural, needed no thought or preparation. He stroked her hair and heard her sigh contentedly. He kissed her, a slow, warm-breathed dance of tongues. He hunted out the softness of her flesh under layers of leather and wool. And at last, jeans and underwear tangled about their ankles, they were joined.

Soon after that, they slept...

Khaled woke, suddenly. There was a sound, there, not there... It grew louder; a vehicle.

"Dawn. Dawn!"

She groaned, muttered, then gasped. "Oh Jesus, can you feel it?"

"We must get out, make for the village." Khaled grabbed her hand and began sliding though the straw towards the entrance to their hiding place.

The vehicle noise became a roar, then the wall shuddered as something slammed against it. Dawn stifled a scream. There was a skittering of… feet, hundreds of feet.

Light pierced the ancient, porous woodwork.

"Are you coming out?" someone shouted, "Or do we let it in?"

"Mike," Dawn sobbed. "It's Mike and…"

Another impact, a clicking sound. Mandibles, Khaled decided. *Huge* mandibles.

"Come on!" Mike yelled. "We only have to open the door and in it comes and, believe you me, it's hungry."

Khaled knew what to do. It was obvious, but it needed courage.

"Stay quiet, Dawn," he whispered, voice so hoarse he could barely frame the words. "I'll give myself up and tell them I'm alo—"

"Shut up, and give me a hand."

Before he could question her, Dawn had scrambled out of their hiding place and was making for the fuel cans. Unsure of what she had in mind, Khaled helped to haul them back to the stack and empty them onto the straw. He gagged on the stench.

"I'm counting," Mike shouted. "Five… Four…"

"Now get by the back door," Dawn produced her lighter. "You'll know when to open it."

"Three… Two…"

Khaled's instinct was to protest, but a hoarse "One!" drove him across to the small rear exit. He began working at the rusty bolt.

The main door exploded inwards in a rage of engine roar and blinding headlight. Wheels spun, the lights drew back, and hell came in.

For a moment, a huge sinuous shape was silhouetted in the glare. There were insectile legs, slashing mandibles, an endless, many-jointed body. Someone screamed, Dawn—

The scream became a flash of a lighter, a loud whoosh, and heat.

Khaled froze, uncomprehending, until flame blotted out the world and

Dawn was pummelling his back with her fists, screeching at him to open the door, open the door, OPEN THE BLOODY DOOR!

The bolt seemed immovable. Heat blasted at his head, seared his face. Smoke slid into his throat and filled his lungs. His struggles became frantic, rusted metal tore his fingers. Then the bolt moved, and Khaled was slamming his shoulder against wood. It jammed; he pushed and pounded and barged.

The door, sunk on its ancient hinges, was ground against the earth. More shoving and wrenching produced a gap and Dawn was out, Khaled close on her heels. They ran, coughing and gasping, into the fire-lit, smoke-fogged dark.

Khaled was in front now, his hand tight around Dawn's as he steered her over ploughed soil towards the high hedge that separated the field from the road.

An engine roared into life. Light swung round the edge of the flames.

Khaled staggered onto the grass headland then slid into the ditch at the foot of the hedge. It was knee-deep with water icy enough to make him gasp with shock. Behind him, Dawn cut off a cry of her own.

He pushed her down into a crouch, then peered over the bank. Headlamps swept the field as Mike's vehicle lurched away from the fire. The light bounced, then stilled, splitting the dark at an odd angle. The engine roared in protest. Doors slammed, men swore.

Legs numb, teeth clattering, Khaled and Dawn moved carefully along the ditch and away from the burning barn and stranded vehicle. The muddy bottom sucked at their feet. The shallow, freezing water seeped upwards through their clothes.

They came to a corner. Khaled stopped for breath. Dawn slumped against him.

"It's my fault they found us." Dawn's voice was tremulous, but whether from cold or fear, Khaled couldn't tell.

"No Dawn..."

"Remember what I told you about the gift."

He did.

"They used the creature to track us down because it could *feel* me."

He held her, stroked her hair. "It does not matter. We have to get away from here."

The engine noise had stopped, replaced by voices. Khaled peered over the bank once more. The barn still burned, tainting the air with smoke. Other lights bobbed across the field, their beams shorter than those from the vehicle lamps. Khaled counted four of them. Torches.

He turned about and tested the hedge. It was dense, and there were thorns. It was impossible to break through.

"I'm freezing, Khaled."

"I know," Khaled grabbed Dawn's hand and they followed the ditch across the front of the approaching torches. "Keep going," he urged. "There must be a gateway soon."

Must there?

The voices were louder now, only a few metres away. Did they have guns? Khaled wondered. Would it be best simply to give in and die quickly, or run, or fight?

Another sound drifted in from the distance, a double-toned siren. The voices became shouts and curses. The torches made a last sweep, then swung away and bobbed quickly back towards the barn.

"Someone's called the fire brigade," Dawn said and started to laugh. "The bloody fire brigade!"

Khaled could not see the joke, but laughed anyway.

~

"You realise that we're on our own." Dawn's voice was loud in the small hours stillness. "I mean, who the hell is going to help a smack-head and an illegal immigrant? And look at the state of us!"

Khaled knew she was right. Both were wet and filthy; no one would believe their story.

The two of them were walking along the lane towards the village, which was still a long way off.

"Where do you think they've gone?" Dawn asked.

"Not far," Khaled said. "They have no transport now. But once we reach the village we will be safe. They would not dare touch us there."

Dawn came to him and burrowed herself under his arm. "I'm scared."

They walked. Khaled shivered and tried to fight his depression. Here he was in a new, safe country, yet still running from those who wanted his life. And all the time he puzzled over why the creatures were being harvested. It was none of his concern, but the question lodged uncomfortably in his mind. He tried to concentrate on the feel of Dawn's hand in his own. It was small and warmed by contact. It seemed trusting, like that of a child.

He stopped and pulled her to himself. She came easily into his arms. He kissed her, in the middle of the road, in the icy dark.

"I love you," Khaled said.

Dawn pulled back from him. "Don't," she said. "Don't ever say that. You don't know me."

Abruptly she walked away, hugging herself, head down. Khaled caught up with her quickly. He tried to stop her, she shrugged off his hand. Desperate now, he danced into her path.

"Stop it, Khaled."

"You must not walk away from me."

She sighed, as if defeated. "Listen to me, Khaled. We need each other just now, but don't lose your heart to me or anything stupid like that. I'm a mess. I'm hurt and angry and I'll make your life hell."

"But I feel—"

"To hell with what you feel." And she was away again.

Khaled followed, but did not try to catch up. Minutes passed.

Then she stopped dead and Khaled almost collided with her.

"Oh Jesus," she breathed. "Oh shit. Oh shit." Her voice was almost a sob. She spun round. "They've sent another one after us."

"Another..."

"It's close. Oh Christ!"

Instinctively Khaled glanced back down the lane, his own terror so deep, so raw, he could barely comprehend it. He grabbed Dawn's hand and made to run. She held back.

"This is useless," she said breathlessly. "We have to split up."

"Split—"

"It's *me*, Khaled. If we split up it will follow me, but not you. You could get to the village, away, they'll never find you."

"No… It will kill you." And how terribly it would kill her. "Dawn, you cannot do this."

Suddenly she was screaming at him. "Run Khaled, run!"

He made to grab her, but she was a fury of feet and claws. She broke away, scrambled onto the bank. Khaled recovered and rushed after her. He glimpsed her, a dark shape against the dark, and drove towards her. There was a violent movement then Khaled reeled back as something slammed into the side of his head. Light exploded in his brain, the world erupted into white pain and the earth slammed into his back.

Dazed, Khaled rolled over and tried to lever himself onto his hands and knees. His limbs gave way and dropped him onto his belly. He laid his cheek against the tarmac. He should sleep, let the dark take him…

He started awake, gritted his teeth and forced himself onto his knees. Another effort and he was on his feet, clutching at his skull, wavering, dizzy, then overwhelmed with nausea. Dawn had hit him hard, with a branch or something he guessed. He reached for the spot tentatively and felt wetness, blood.

The light was greying into dawn now.

Dawn…

He couldn't let it happen. He saw a gateway; beyond was yet another field, this one planted with rows of thick-leafed root crops. Some of the plants were broken, stamped down. Not much of a trail, but indicating that someone had been this way. Khaled set off across the field, following the crushed crops towards a break in the far hedge.

He prayed as he ran, cried out to Allah for Dawn's life and wondered why God should listen to someone as faithless as he. The prayer became a chant, rhythmed with each footfall, until he burst through the gap and saw her.

Dawn, standing in the middle of this second field, hugging herself, head bowed. She had given up. Khaled could tell, even from this distance.

She stiffened, her head snapped up. She took a step back, another.

It was coming. It was close.

Khaled plunged into the field, chest on fire, head a storm of pain. Dawn didn't see him until he was almost on her. She half-turned and before she could protest, Khaled had her arm and was dragging her towards the field's gateway.

There was a road beyond it, but no help. No help at all.

Dawn screamed. Khaled glanced back and saw the creature erupt out of the hedgerow on the far side of the field; a rage of blind, violent instinct and relentless hunger, hurtling towards them at an impossible speed. Adrenalin surged through him, pain became meaningless.

He plunged through the gate.

A second backward glance revealed the creature framed in the gap. Khaled shouted at Dawn, telling her to run, run, RUN! She stumbled away, along the lane. Khaled staggered in pursuit, but all his strength had gone. It was over.

Chitinous feet scratched at tarmac. Something roared. He spun round. Saw...

A lorry, vast and silhouetted behind its own glaring headlamps.

The creature reared, lunged, then shattered into a thousand bloody fragments.

Brakes screeched, tyres slithered and the lorry skewed to a halt.

~

Silence.

So intense, it was almost a roar.

The lorry was motionless in the middle of the narrow road, its engine stopped, its grill and windscreen smeared with juices and gore.

Khaled, struggling to breathe, dizzy with an odd meld of euphoria and shock, was on his knees in front of the vehicle. He was alive, the creature was dead, utterly destroyed, fragments of its jointed body and legs strewn about the road and the verge. He knew he should move, should do something, but he could only stand up, shakily, and concentrate on breathing.

He became aware of Dawn, who was standing fifty or so metres away. Her mouth was open but no sound emerged.

The click of the lorry's door broke the white silence. It swung open and a large, squat man with long dark hair dropped down onto the road accompanied by a snatch of loud heavy metal. He shook his head, looked round. It seemed to take a while for him to focus on Khaled.

"What the fuck was that?" he said, then appeared to recover a little. "It was chasing you." He made it sound like an accusation.

"We were walking, it came..." Khaled thickened his accent to fog his explanation.

The driver studied him hard, and Khaled realised he was filthy and wet, not like somebody who had just been walking. The driver looked dubious as he reached into his jacket pocket. In a moment he was stabbing at the screen of his iPhone.

"Police," he said.

Police; questions, arrest and expulsion.

"Yes, it is a bloody emergency. I've hit something... no, I don't know what it is. Fuck's sake, there's bits of it all over my lorry... What? It was fucking huge..."

Khaled spun round and broke into a run. His legs were heavy. He was too tired for this, but he couldn't stay. He had to get way, from the police, back into the town and his cousins.

"Oi! Where're you going?" The driver, shouting, but not following. "No, no not you, there's a foreign bastard and a woman, in the road. Yeah hell of a state..."

Khaled grabbed Dawn's arm as he ran past. She stumbled in his wake, shouting and protesting.

"Can't we ride in the lorry... Khaled... for God's sake, I'm exhausted..."

Khaled ran on, gasping for air now. Cold air burned his throat. And suddenly, he was tired of running and hiding. It had been the same since he was in Afghanistan, running, always running.

A vehicle, coming fast. Khaled yanked Dawn down to the left onto the verge. They went down on their bellies in the wet grass. Khaled looked up and saw a car burst round the corner. Police. He put his head back down as the car rushed by. Air ruffled the grass. For a moment, all was roar and siren then it faded, quietened.

Wearily, Khaled got back to his feet pulling Dawn up with him. He felt her hand close about his and found some comfort there.

"I told you I'd make your life hell," she said.

~

About half an hour later they came to a village. The place seemed to consist of a single street with a church, pub and a shop that acted as grocer, newsagent and supermarket.

A helicopter rattled overhead, low and fast. Khaled looked up and saw that it was painted military green.

They crossed to the shop. Dawn went in first, to explain away their damp and filth as a result of a car accident and their need for phone credit to call for some assistance.

A moment later she beckoned Khaled to follow. There was a girl serving at the counter, already smart in her school uniform. Her eyes were wide and she looked frightened.

Newspaper headlines caught Khaled's eye. The massacres in Africa and the former Soviet republic still dominated the front pages. Bodies torn, half-eaten...

A car drew up, white, decorated with an orange flash. A police constable climbed out. Khaled quickly moved to the back of the shop where Dawn was grabbing ice cream cartons from the freezer. She looked up just as the door jangled open, then clutched Khaled's arm and pulled him round and out of sight.

"Morning Jan," the constable said cheerily. "One Mail and one Mirror, thanks love."

Khaled glimpsed the newspapers, those headlines and photographs again.

Then understood.

He pulled away from Dawn.

"Where are you going?" she hissed at him.

He did not believe in silence. His father had not stayed silent and paid the price.

Khaled touched her face, briefly. "I know what the Eggs are harvested for."

"No," Dawn sounded desolate. "No... please. It's none of our business. They'll send you back."

Khaled's voice was hoarse. "I cannot run away anymore. Too many people will die."

"Well fuck you," Dawn sobbed. "Fuck you to hell."

Not trusting himself to look at her, wanting her with him but unable to stop now, Khaled forced himself across the shop. The constable was at the door, about to step outside.

"Excuse me," Khaled called out. The constable paused. "My name is Khaled Khan and I must speak with you." He picked up a newspaper and held its front page towards the constable, who had turned in the doorway. "This..." He struggled for the right words. "I know who..."

For a second, the officer hesitated, but then started back into the shop as his eyes suddenly flicked from Khaled's to focus on something over his shoulder. Before Khaled could turn to see what it was, Dawn slipped her hand into his.

"Yeah, me too," she said, looking up at Khaled with a resigned smile, then to the officer. "We've got something very important to tell you."

Journey to the Engine of the Earth

We stand on a grassed, wind-lashed slope that borders the Lemon Way estate.

"So," I say to The Visitor. "Exactly where do you want to go?"

I don't want to look at The Visitor because the hood of its parka is down. The Visitor still disturbs me, it disturbs all of us. It isn't local. Its home, as far as we've been able to work out, is a moon that orbits a gas giant in the Beta Ophiuchus system.

"That way," the Visitor says and waves towards the three, night-blackened tower blocks that dominate the estate. Its voice is husky, throaty, like someone who has smoked their vocal chords to shreds. "To the centre." To my relief it pulls up its hood and fades into parka-esque anonymity.

"Okay," I call out. "Time to move."

The others, my team I suppose you'd call them, are huddled together off to my left. I don't know what actually qualifies me to be their leader. My name is John Chamberlain and I'm a dentist, not an explorer.

But The Visitor has picked me as leader so leader I am.

The Visitor picked the whole team in fact, selecting the six of us from a thousand, thousand sets of CVs, medical records, bank statements and any other information available to brush-stroke our characters and lives. The selections it made seem random and bizarre. None of us are volunteers. We were politely but firmly roused from our beds by people who looked like police officers but weren't and brought before a panel of grim-faced men and women in some generic office in what I presume was London. The van that ferried us there had no windows.

We were introduced to our Visitor and, once we had calmed down, informed that there are about five hundred of them scattered all over the Earth and God knows how many more living on their continent-sized vessel, waiting up there in geostationary orbit directly above the Great Pyramid at Cheops. Coincidence or connection? Who knows. All we do know is that their hardware is bigger and much more intimidating than anything we've got. They have asked for help in finding the Engine of the Earth and help they will be given.

Few people know about this, not even the police or army are aware. So, mouths shut and mobile phones off. There will be no calling for help if things go wrong. There was no time for any training. Two days in a hotel to get to know each other, some powerful torches and a map of the estate and that's it.

Their time-synchronised search, which begins now, will take the Visitors and their human teams into the worst places imaginable; war zones, areas wracked by natural or manmade disaster, slums and the most dangerous council estate in this country. The Visitors have given no clues as to the nature of this Engine although they have promised that when they do find it, they will simply disappear and leave us alone. Current thinking identifies it as the indomitable human spirit, survival in adversity, a sign that humanity has some worth and is not interstellar vermin. So, I'm expecting our particular quest into the desolation of Lemon Valley to uncover a courageous single-mum or heroic youth worker.

Paul speaks first. He is a big, broad, head-shaved ex-infantryman, bundled, like the rest of us, into an obligatory parka. Paul intimidates me but I'm glad he's here. I wish he'd been picked as leader.

"I'll stay at the back, keep an eye on our flank," he says. "If there's any trouble up front I'll come running."

Seems like a good idea to me.

We form into a ragged line and descend the slope via a set of rain-slippery concrete steps. The Visitor is in front of me. At my shoulder is a Cabinet Minister named Katherine Kristian. She has not been friendly and only grudgingly co-operative. I suppose she thinks she should be the leader.

Behind Katherine is Rajan Uppal, who works in Sainsbury's or Tesco's or somewhere similar. He's affable enough, and utterly terrified, though trying his best to hide the fact. Between Rajan and Paul is a High School maths teacher called Rachel Goldman. She's the one who is taking this seriously and, as far as I can see, the bravest member of Chamberlain's Marauders.

At the bottom of the stairway, we move carefully into a cut between two high grassy banks. I feel vulnerable down here. Katherine moves up beside me. "You okay?" Is this genuine concern or politics?

I nod. "What about you?"

"This seems so surreal," she says. "And this place...God knows what it must be like to live here."

"Perhaps that's what we're supposed to find out."

She nods. "You think that's what the Engine is? Humans beings forced to confront the suffering of others?"

It sounds like a speech. Embarrassed I shrug a noncommittal shrug.

The cut takes us into an underpass, which stinks of booze and piss. There are lights, though most of them are broken. In the sickly patches of illumination they do provide I see graffiti; gang boasts and threats, sexual insults, favours offered. The gibberish on the walls heightens my sense that this is the homeland of a completely separate species almost as alien as The Visitor itself.

The cut curves out of the underpass and slopes steadily upwards. I hear music. It is relentless, monotonous, some way off but malevolent enough. Someone shouts, the voice lonely, reverberating off the slab-like concrete walls of the tower blocks that now loom over us. There is a snatch of laughter, male. More shouting, glass shatters.

"You do know that there were five murders on this estate last year," Rajan informs us as we walk. He sounds nervous.

"In this area," Rachel corrects him. "They were not all on the estate."

"That's all right then," Rajan says and chuckles. There isn't much humour in the sound.

There are buildings on either side of us, squat and soulless. Each one is three storeys high and flat-roofed. Light spills from their curtain-concealed windows. I stop the team to consult the map, struggling to keep it flat in the rain-edged wind.

"Left," I say and hope I'm right because it feels as if we've entered a maze. The music grows louder, mingles with other nihilistic beats, fades and is replaced by more. Shrieks and shouts erupt from one of the blocks. A door slams.

Figures emerge from the shadows to our right and run across our path. I tense, not knowing whether to order a retreat or a stand. The figures move on and disappear. There is breathless laughter, male, mocking. A car erupts out of the half-dark, headlights blaze white. It hurtles past, all engine roar, exhaust stink and pulsing, skull-fracturing music. It brakes and wheel-spins behind us then swerves right and is gone. We're being watched, from the flats, from the pools of dark the street lighting cannot penetrate. I can feel it, eyes raking my skin, flaying it to the raw nerves beneath.

We press on until we reach the edge of a large, open area bordered on each of its three sides by a trio of tower blocks. They rear over us, looking as if they have erupted out of the earth rather than been built. Light punctuates their blank, brutalist frontages. They each have a name; Emerson, Lake and Palmer, which proves that there is a developer in this world who either nurses a lingering love for prog rock or is blessed with a sense of humour. I suspect the latter. Some sort of statue or sculpture sits in the middle of the area.

Another look at the map. "That thing's supposed to be the actual centre of this shit hole," I say.

"Don't call it that." Katherine sounds as if she means it.

"Why not, that's what it is," Rajan says.

"Names like that aren't helpful," Katherine tells him.

"So you think this is paradise then?"

"Don't be stupid Rajan."

"That's enough," I say and although my rebuke sounds weak both of them stop.

"What is that thing?" Rachel asks.

"Fuck knows, looks like a big lump of concrete to me," Rajan says.

"That because you're a Philistine," Rachel tells him.

"A what?"

"I think the piece is a Gormley," Katherine says.

"Oh," says Rajan but I don't think he's any wiser.

"Is that where we're supposed to go?" I ask The Visitor.

It turns its hood-hidden face towards me. "Yes."

"Is that where the engine is?"

"Perhaps."

There is a problem.

Several cars are parked close together about halfway between us the sculpture. Drum and Bass, or whatever it's called, throbs from the speakers in one of the hatchbacks. Even from this distance each beat is a punch to the stomach. Car-light and street light silhouette the characters lounging and playing around the cars into demonic figures, capering about the bonfires of Hell. There is something primitive about them, like the natives in some clichéd old Hollywood Tarzan film.

"Is there a way to the sculpture that doesn't involve crossing that triangle?" Katherine must be telepathic because I'm already unfolding the map.

I fumble with the flapping sheet of paper and my torch. I can't think for the noise.

"Let me have a look," says Paul. Logical idea, except I don't want him to. I'm supposed to be the leader, I'm supposed to get us to our destination. I fumble on.

"Oh for God's sake." Katherine snatches the map out of my hand. It tears. "Paul, come and do this will you."

I'm angry, but Paul is already peering at the diagram so protest seems futile at that moment.

"There's a path that leads round the back of the Emerson," he says.

"Let's go then," Katherine says.

"I don't know." Why am I doing this? Caution or pride?

"I do," says Rachel. "We're asking for trouble if we attempt to cross the triangle. We should go Paul's way and take our chances."

I want her to shut up and stay out of this. I want them all to keep quiet. I can't think for the noise.

"What about you Rajan?" Katherine asks.

"I'm not walking through that lot." Rajan nods towards the car tribe.

The mutiny is complete. I glance at The Visitor. No help there.

"Fuck," I mutter.

"What?" Rachel says.

"You win," I say. "You'd better lead, Paul. I'll watch the rear."

We enter yet another maze of narrow walkways and car-lined streets, all edged by low, cubist blocks. There's a pub, no different from the faceless concrete lumps around it. A group of smokers huddle outside. I catch a hint of wind-blown tobacco exhaust. The smokers watch us as we pass, no one speaks.

I notice that Katherine has moved up beside Paul, no doubt assuming her natural position in the order of things.

We turn a corner and blunder to a halt.

The street is like most others on the estate; concrete, tarmac, rubbish-strewn and all illuminated by orange street-light. But this one includes a large people carrier with blacked-out windows, idling by the pavement about ten metres away. A cluster of figures are gathered round it and it looks as if money is changing hands. The group are made anonymous by the abysmal light but I can almost taste their malevolence.

Drug deal. What else can it be?

And here we are, a clutch of strangers, only a few metres away, frozen like rabbits in car headlights.

"We have to go back," I move up to the front.

"No we don't," Katherine says. "We just cross over and walk past. They're not interested in us."

"We have to find another route," Rachel says. Even she sounds scared now.

"I think John's right," Rajan says.

"He's not. He's over-reacting," Katherine says. "We're too close to where we want to get to. I mean, do you really want to trudge all the way back?"

"Paul?" I say. I'm uneasy. The gang have seen us. They're glancing this way.

"Don't mind. Whatever you want to do boss," he says and shrugs.

"We're going back."

"It's too far." Katherine is mounting a leadership challenge. "Everyone is cold and tired and we just want to get this whole thing over with so we can go home.

"The Visitor appointed me as leader." No, no, wrong. I should not have said that, too weak, too pleading. But there isn't time for niceties, this place is closing in on me. I'm breathing too fast, shaking. I press on with my defence against Katherine's coup. "And I say we go back."

Rajan nods, Rachel moves in towards me. I've done it. I've beaten down the insurgency. Now we need to get out of here because these characters and their blacked-out people carrier and huddled, dark whispering and dealing is scaring the hell out of me...

"Hey! What the fuck you lookin' at?" The voice is deep. And aggressive.

They're coming. Dear God, they're coming after us.

Something breaks inside me and I run. I think I shout at the others to do the same but I can't remember. All I know is that I have to get out of there. This is fear, real fear, not stage fright or some extreme sport adrenalin rush, this is survival-fear. It forces a sob from my throat, it pumps my legs and arms and snatches away my breath.

The pub, I have to get to the pub, light, people. No one is going to gun me down in front of so many witnesses. Are they? Well, are they? Witnesses keep their mouths shut in places like this? No one sees anything. All the Lemon Way murders are unsolved...

My team, Jesus, my team, my people.

I can't stop for them. I can't stop for anything.

The pub comes into view. I look over my shoulder. No sign of the drug dealers. They thought we were the police, they've driven away. They're racing through some short cut intent on heading us off...

My team appear, running, together, a group, a family. And here I am, away out front, the so-called leader, first off the blocks when danger rears its head.

Ashamed I stumble to a halt and wait, panting, hands on knees. The pub smokers regard me curiously. A woman laughs. Someone coughs and spits.

We're back where we started, crouching between Emerson and Lake, watching the gang who we will have to pass to get to our – The Visitor's – destination. There is no other way. The others have separated themselves from me and who can blame them? I left them, ran away and deserted my post. No one has criticised me openly. No one has confronted me but it's there, unspoken yet deafening.

I can't tell what The Visitor feels about my failure.

"They're just kids," I say, nodding towards the car tribe that is blocking our way to the sculpture.

If I say it enough times I might believe it myself...

No one answers, no discussion so no point staying here.

"Let's go," I say and gritting my teeth, set off across the triangle. Everyone follows. Their obedience thrums with resentment.

Halfway across we're noticed. The music punches into my gut. I see figures detach themselves from the cars. I'm struck by their gauntness, their pale, pinched faces, their hunched backs, the degenerate, somehow mutated look of them, as if they have been bred into the shape and demeanour best suited for this environment. Their clothes are alien too, slovenly and cheap looking, no style or shape, but a uniform nonetheless. The shouting starts. It's not a challenge, not a demand to know who we are. They are shouting at the women; filth, obscene propositions. I hate their mindless cackle and I hate their wasted pasty skin and stupid bloody clothes and vile bloody music and my hate speeds my heart rate and drains the blood from my brain until my head roars.

"Come on lads, that's enough." Rachel's tone is non-threatening yet authoritative.

A bottle smashes on the path just ahead of me. They move away from their cars and prance, apelike, around us. Another bottle smashes. But no violence, not yet.

I keep walking, and the others are with me. I want to run, but I have to atone.

The taunting goes on; suck this, feel that. On and bloody on. A third bottle lands somewhere behind me. No one cries out, no one hurt.

One of them comes in close. He's a light-built, hyperactive little shit. He walks alongside Katherine. "Hey," Paul says. "Leave her alone."

The lad is fast, leaps out of Paul's reach in an instant. His manoeuvre is cheered by the others. Katherine keeps walking, head down, face set. The quick one darts in again.

And Katherine snaps, her rage a deafening screech of tears and fury.

"Shut up. Fucking shut up! Shut up, shut up shut up..."

One of them mimics her.

"You heard her, piss off!" Paul is at them now, his patience gone. He's shouting, spittle flies "Piss off you worthless little shits."

The laughter stops. One of them moves in on Paul.

"Who you talkin' to?" he says.

"You, you worthless little cunt."

"Paul, no," Rachel seems to claw her way towards the face-off with dreamlike slowness. Everyone is shouting. I freeze.

Because I don't know what to do.

Rachel grabs at Paul, but it's too late. He's pushed the youth so hard the kid has fallen over. Paul drops to his knees. His arm pistons; down, up, down, up. Each descending stroke ends in a soft, fleshy thud.

The gang mill around. They shout; "Fuck, oh Christ, he's fucking killing him!" And their voices are full of terror, and yet at the same time some of them laugh. One of them pauses long enough to take photos with his phone then he bounces backwards shouting at his mates to wait for him. Another is being held back. He screams with rage, howls threats, struggles in his mates' arms then breaks away and runs. He has a pattern shaved into his close-cropped hair, a zig-zag that runs along the side of his scalp.

Paul stops and slowly, almost painfully gets to his feet. He stares down at his work, motionless now. Rachel stands beside him. Her hand goes to her mouth. It seems to take me a thousand years to reach the group. The youth is curled on the ground. I can't see any details, only the black lake of blood that reaches out and around his head. Katherine kneels beside him, Rachel is clinging to Rajan's arm. I crouch beside Katherine and notice her perfume and how sensual it is and then wonder at how I can be aroused by a woman's scent while crouched beside someone a member of my team has just beaten almost to death.

"We have to get help," Katherine says.

I shake my head. "We can't." My voice is barely audible even to myself.

Katherine is demanding my attention and demanding that I get help. How? We haven't got any phones. We are supposed to support The Visitor at all costs. That's what we are told by the men and women in sharp and shiny suits. The needs of the many outweigh the needs of the individual.

I become aware that Paul is kneeling again. He's shaking. It doesn't take much imagination to work out why. He was a soldier for Christ's sake. I'm scared shitless now because the big dependable ex-infantryman who watched our flanks is actually suffering from some post-traumatic stress or other and seems to be in the grip of a panic attack.

Katherine has restarted her litany about getting help. Rajan says that she's right. I want them all to shut up. I want them all to get off my back and shut up.

I stumble over to The Visitor and shove my face into its impassive, inscrutable mask and yell. "What do you want? What the fuck do you want? Why don't you help us? "

"I want to find the Engine of the Earth," it answers and I want to hit the vile bloody thing but I don't because I'm too frightened.

I back away, look round and see everyone staring at me; silent, appalled, scornful.

"We're going to find a phone and get help," Rachel says. By we, she obviously means herself and Rajan. She is holding his arm.

I shake my head. "No, we have to stay together."

"We can't do that John." Katherine is using her best patronising-politician's tone. "That boy is badly hurt. We can't let him die." She draws me apart. "Don't you think it wise to show ourselves as creatures of compassion?" She glances at The Visitor as if to emphasise her point.

I've failed. My team is breaking up. I'm going to be the one slammed by the media when all this finally emerges from the shadows.

"Paul." I snap. "Paul we have to go." He ignores me, sits down, head bowed.

"Paul!"

"For Christ's sake John," Katherine shouts at me. "We can't go. Don't you understand? We have to help this boy."

"Okay, do what you bloody want?" I yell so loudly the words tear my throat. "Do what you think is best, don't let me stand in your way. That...That little bastard deserved what he got."

I swing round and take a step towards the sculpture.

And someone bursts out of the dark. He's shouting and screaming. I see the zig-zag razored into his hair. I see the gun in his hand.

He's out of control. The gun swings around wildly and we're all frozen in place. The slightest pressure on that trigger and someone will be hurt. The youth rants, calls us murderers and filth. The others draw together, and withdraw from me. No one orders it, they just do, the action unconscious and brutal. Even Paul is part of the group and he caused this.

I have to do something. It's my role, I'm leader here. I have to confront the youth and take the gun. I have to show some worth, some act of courage to put things right.

Rachel is talking to him, so quietly I can't hear what's she's saying. She takes a step towards him, arms away from her sides, hands open. She snags the boy's attention, for a moment, long enough...

I lurch forwards, stumble against the youth, who feels surprisingly thin and small and light, and make a grab for the weapon. I hear shouts and cries and then an explosion, shocking, loud and illuminated by a dazzling flash of light.

The silence is worse.

The kid is on the ground. He scuttles back, mouth open and whimpering. I look round and see that someone else is down. Rachel. Down and still and, like Paul's victim, haloed in something dark and spreading. I grope my way towards her and feel an object under my palm.

"The gun," I say. "It's okay, I have the gun..."

It isn't okay. Nothing is okay. Sound returns, crying and shouting.

I look up to see The Visitor. Its hood is down. Something resembling a smile is screwed into its face.

"Thank you," it says.

Then I hear a police siren, growing louder. People are emerging from the flats and finally I understand what has happened here and why everyone is crying and howling and that, somehow it's my fault.

I also realise that The Visitor has gone.

Sunday...

The first I know of it is when I switch on the van's radio and find the usual small hours easy listening replaced by the solemn tones of a newscaster. There's been no comment from the Palace yet.

The *Palace*?

Then it's over to Geoffrey Haines at the crash site where members of the rescue services are still picking through the smouldering wreckage of rock singer Jude Ellerton's light aircraft. There are no survivors.

The pieces slot together... Christ.

Laura opens the front door to me when I arrive home. She's in her nightdress, and looks pale. I think she's been crying. "Have you heard?" she says. "Princess Joanna..."

There are hours of it, on every television channel; facts, eulogies, speculation, round and round, over and over, until, glutted, I switch it off.

Outraged, our teenage daughter Rebecca flees to her room.

Later, I wash my van, which has to double as our family car because times are hard for the self-employed electrician. Dave Hill emerges from number 52. He's wearing some kind of tracksuit which was never designed for someone of his size and age.

"I'm surprised to see you out here, Tim," he says

I turn off the hose. "Moping in front of the telly won't bring Joanna back,"

He tells me I'm callous, then snaps; "She should never have got herself mixed up with that bastard Ellerton. He duped her, played her innocence."

"Joanna's *innocence?*"

"You shouldn't speak ill of the dead, Steve,"

"You called her a Right Royal Tart once."

"I don't think I did," Dave says. And there's something in his voice that warns me not to argue any further. So I swig Ruddles and turn the hose back on.

"Perhaps you should forget the van today, Tim."

I turn it off again. No point upsetting the neighbours.

After lunch, Laura and I go for a walk. There are few people around, and anyone we do meet averts their eyes, as if ashamed to be out on the day Joanna died.

Monday...

The world stands still, scarcely daring to breathe.

Tuesday...

Laura works late, comes home at around eight, tired and exasperated. "God," she says, slumping down at the dining room table. "Now the management want us to wear those black armbands the newspapers are giving away."

I glance at Rebecca, who is sporting just such an accessory. "It's a sign of respect," she pipes up, right on cue.

"I know, sweetheart," Laura says wearily. "But it's a free country and I don't want to wear an armband just because some tabloid tells me to." Rebecca doesn't answer, but goes back to her homework. I serve Laura the dinner I've cooked her.

The doorbell chimes.

It's Dave and his wife, Elaine.

I invite them in and notice that both are wearing arm bands.

"This isn't entirely a social visit," Dave says portentously while Elaine sniffs into a tissue. "I'm sure you've aware that Joanna's funeral is to be on Saturday,"

We are, of course.

"Well, we, that is the residents of The Close, have decided to club together to hire a coach so we can attend. We're planning to leave at about three am so we're there in good time."

"It's the least we can do," says Elaine.

"I'm sorry but I can't make it," I say. "Laura and Rebecca might want to come though."

"And why can't *you* come, Tim?"

"I'm on a weekend call-out rota. I was reserve last weekend, first call this week."

"You could swap with someone," Elaine manages through her tears.

"We don't mess about with the rota."

"I won't be coming either," Laura says quietly. "I like to be here for Tim on first call weekends."

Dave shakes his head, a slow, deliberate motion. "I have to say that I'm very disappointed in you both. I find your attitude quite antisocial, callous even."

Wednesday...

Posters are tied to all the lamp posts in The Close, identical, depicting Joanna staring, Che Guevara-like, into the far distance.

On television, a pale, drawn Monarch utters carefully chosen platitudes.

Stones have been thrown, at the Palace, at the windows of shops due to open on Saturday; people are injured. The tabloids have coined a name for the victims. NMs – Non Mourners.

"Rebecca," I say quietly. "I don't want you to go on Saturday."

"But Dad—"

"It's too dangerous. Look at the television."

She doesn't. She shouts and howls, then flees upstairs.

"That was a good idea," Laura snaps as she makes to go after her.

"Surely it's only a minority making trouble."

Thursday...

Laura meets me at the front door. "You'd better go upstairs," she says coldly. I do as I'm told. Rebecca, still in her school uniform, is on the bed, her back to me.

"Go away," she snarls.

I touch her shoulder. Her foetal curl tightens. "Come on Rebecca, please tell me what happened."

She twists over, revealing a bruised cheek and swollen eye.

"They said I'm an NM bitch!" she screams. "I'm not. I *loved* Joanna. I loved her so much." Anger crumbles into sobbing.

"But you didn't," I say stupidly, calm through my rage at my daughter's hurts. "Don't you understand? You *liked* her, you *admired* her, but you didn't *love* her. It's the newspapers Rebecca." Is it? I change tack. "Who did this to you?"

No answer, only sobs.

"You should let her go," Laura tells me when I go downstairs.

"No, I'm sorry."

"Dave and Elaine will look after her."

"On their side now, are you?"

"They're our neighbours, for God's sake, our friends. Don't you remember?"

"No, I don't. I'm going to the school."

She laughs, bitterly. "I've done that already. The head master said that 'feelings are running high' and that it was basically our own fault."

Something breaks. And I'm storming outside, slamming the front door. I stride to the nearest lamppost and tear down its Joanna poster, ripping it into as many pieces as I can manage, letting the wind spiral the fragments across The Close.

I notice a figure, standing under the lamp outside a nearby house, a neighbour, John Bartlett the policeman, face hidden in shadow, but watching.

I'm alone in the lounge, television off, radio silent, when the doorbell chimes.

Dave steps into the hall without invitation. "You bastard!" he shouts, and shakes a handful of poster fragments in my face. "You callous, unfeeling, bastard."

"I think you'd better go home," I say with a calmness that shocks me because I want to take him by the throat.

"I thought you were my friend," Dave grinds out. "But all you can do is trample over our feelings. Elaine is distraught about this. I've a fucking good mind to—"

"Get out."

Dave looks up, past my shoulder and splutters to a halt. I spin round to see Laura on the landing.

"How dare you burst in here threatening my husband," she grinds out. "I've a good mind to call the police..."

"I wouldn't do that if I were you." Bartlett steps out of the dark and into the open doorway. "My colleagues won't take kindly to this kind of heartless vandalism." He places a hand on Dave's shoulder. "Come on, they're not worth it. Let's go home."

I hold Laura close. She's shaking, but not crying. I stroke her hair and tell her she was brave. I'm shaking as well. So I tighten my hold, as much for my own comfort as hers.

Friday...

More buildings burn, someone dies. The Prime Minister calls for calm.

There's a parcel on the doorstep when I get home from work. I take it indoors and drop it onto the dining room table. Laura is at the oven. Rebecca is watching television. I trudge upstairs for a shower, glad to be home, relieved that nothing has happened. We'll lock the doors early tonight. Close down, hide. One more day to go until...what? Normality?

"Tim! Oh God, TIM!"

The stench hits me before I reach the dining room. Hits me and makes me gag.

Laura is standing back from the table, hands over her mouth, sobbing. Rebecca is on her feet, ashen, shaking. The parcel contained a box, now open to reveal a churned mass of cat excrement. There's a letter – the words cut from newspapers and magazines, ransom note style.

YOu'Re goING tO buRn in hell you NM fuckeRs.

Laura spins away to vomit into the kitchen sink. My own stomach twists, but rage conquers disgust. I scoop the thing up and crash out of the house. I make for Dave's, then change my mind and deposit the parcel in my own dustbin. I've got to stay calm tonight, for my wife and daughter's sake.

When I return, the house smells of detergent, bleach and air freshener, though the stink is still there, ground into our nostrils, impregnating the air, the walls.

Not much later, Laura and I lay on the bed, fully dressed, holding each other. I switch out the light. Laura moves closer.

Saturday...

A sound jars me awake. I'm disorientated, stale and crumpled in my clothes. The sound is an engine, diesel, big, entering The Close. Headlights sweep our bedroom. Air brakes hiss, the engine growl drops to a rhythmic pulse. I reach for Laura...

And hear a creak on the stairs.

Another creak, further down.

I'm scramble out of the bed, stumble across the darkened bedroom, onto the landing. I fumble for the light switch, see the front door close, glimpse a coat-bundled figure.

"Rebecca!" I shout and clatter downstairs, outside.

Where there is nothing but yellow-white, and dark shapes gathered about the coach. I charge them, calling my daughter's name.

A missile arcs towards me, broken brick, thudding on the pavement at my feet. Another slams into my right shoulder, the pain explosive and shocking. The coach roars and lurches forward. I hear Laura screaming as I stumble backwards and fall into our flower border.

Wheels crunch, the sky is blotted out. There is noise, light, the stink of oil and exhaust. Then it stops, roars again and wrenches itself backwards. More bricks. I hear glass shatter.

The coach roars for a third time, yellow-white turns blood red, the sound lingers, then fades until, apart from Laura's quiet sobbing, The Close is silent.

We watch the funeral, huddled in our lounge, now darkened to permanent night by the sheet of plywood I've nailed over the window our neighbours broke.

Westminster Abbey is packed with celebrity, power and wealth. Jude Ellerton's brother delivers a scarcely disguised anti-royal eulogy that sends cold shivers through the church, and a ripple of mindless applause through the crowds outside. Then the remains of Ellerton's boyband sing a specially adapted version of one of their hits. Two of them break down in tears during the second chorus.

We don't move until long after it is finished. There are newsflashes; buildings burn, mobs hunt. The police are warning people to stay indoors unless their journeys are absolutely necessary.

I make coffee and toast cheese, edgy. The false dark inside melds with the real dark outside.

The phone rings.

"It's a job," I say. "Look, I'll call someone else, tell them I'm already out—"

"No," Laura answers. "I want you to go."

I protest, but she is adamant. It's a matter of principle. So I kiss her, pull on my jacket and leave the house. An icy breeze slaps my face and bothers the Princess Joanna posters on their lampposts. As I reverse the van out of the garage and down the drive, I know fear, real fear, probably, for the first time in my life. My joints ache, I shake uncontrollably.

The job, a heating breakdown, is at an old peoples' home. The frail residents are gathered in the lounge, where a portable gas fire hisses and the television shows a repeat of the funeral.

The fault eludes me. My fingers are stiff and awkward, my brain slow.

The system is ancient, basic. I probe and trace, barely controlling my panic. I want, I *must* get home before the coach comes back.

I find a burnt-out relay. From the lounge comes the sound of a hymn, the voices lost in the enormity of Westminster Abbey. I begin disconnecting wires. My mobile phone warbles. Then stops, abruptly. "Missed call. Home." *Home*, the word short yet terrifying. I dial back, tucking it under my chin to free my hands.

No answer. Ringing though, on and on, but no answer.

And I'm running, leaving my tool bag behind and the old folks shivering.

The streets are smoke-fogged, flame-lit. There is broken glass, upturned cars, bundles on the ground, that look like... Jesus, surely not...

When I reach The Estate I'm slowed by a crowd, heading in the same direction as me. There's a party mood. Laughter, shouting.

I swing into The Close.

Which is jammed with people, A house is burning, several. One of them...

Mine.

Christ oh Christ. *Mine*.

I ram open the van door. Shouting, losing control. No one hears me, there's too much noise. And stench... more than burning wood and paint. Something else, petrol, scorched clothing, roasting meat.

That's when I see the other, smaller fires, raging about a number of the lampposts, engulfing things that move, that writhe and live, however briefly.

"NM," shouts the crowd.

"Laura!" I scream and begin pushing my way through the crowd which closes behind me. "Laura LAURAAAAH!"

But my voice is lost among the others, Laura's name swamped and dissolved.

"NM!" they chant, on and fucking on. "ENEM, ENEMENEMENEM..."

As well as writing, Terry teaches, acts and directs, and is a regular harmonica player and vocalist at "Aint Nothin' But The Blues" open mic Sunday afternoon jams in London. He is the author of five novels and novellas: *Shadow Waltz: Soul Masque Parts 1 and 2*, *The Places Between*, *Axe*, *Bloody War* and *Deadside Revolution*. His short stories have appeared in a variety of magazines and anthologies over the years. He has also written and directed three plays: *The Bayonet*, *Tattletale Mary* and *The Friends of Mike Santini*, and contributed and co-written a number of engineering and electrical text books. He runs theEXAGGERATEDpress and Wordland magazine.